I0545007

B Cyde Books presents

Reaching the Edge of Merci:

Fruit of a Dead Tree

Written By: Dawn Crooks

Reaching the Edge of Merci: Fruit of a Dead Tree

Written By: Dawn L. Crooks

Edited By: Tracie E. Christian

Published By: B Cyde Books LLC

Cover Design/Layout: Regina Poole

Author Photo: Nzingha Byrd

This book is published under the Copyright Laws of the United States of America

No part of this book may be used, reproduced, stored in a retrieval system, or transmitted in any form, by any means, electronic, mechanical, photocopying recording or otherwise without the expressed written consent/permission of Dawn L. Crooks

Printed in the United States

ISBN – 13: 978-1-7356375-0-1

ACKNOWLEDGEMENTS

I am ever grateful for the artistic community for holding me up and always encouraging me to reach for my next artistic level. They have been family for as long as I can remember. They have patiently awaited the arrival of this series. I hope I do them proud with this, my first attempt at authorship.

I am ever grateful for the highly skilled writers that my college studies introduced to my world; Toni Morrison, James Baldwin, Pearl Cleage, William Faulkner, Jean Rhys, Zora Neale Hurston, August Wilson, and Alice Walker to name a few. They gave me a bar to reach for. I don't know if I will get there, but the journey to discover how high I could go has been one I will never regret.

I am every grateful for my publisher, Tracie E. Christian. As my friend, she has loved me for a long time. As my sista', she has walked with me through times of doubt. As my creative peer, she has always called on me to grace the stages her own artistic career built. There is no one else who I would have trusted to guide me through this process and to take care of the baby I was afraid to let fly.

And finally, I am ever grateful for the gift that the Creator saw fit to bless me with. Destiny has a way of driving energy. This energy would not let me rest

until I put it to page and let it live. I humbly offer
every word back to the divine place from which it
was birthed.

TABLE OF CONTENTS

FORWARD

Growing up in a Black home meant keeping secrets. We all lived by the mantra that what happened in our homes stayed in our homes. It didn't matter if dysfunction was being allowed to fester. I always wondered why and how this became a universal understanding. Was it fear? Had we been stigmatized enough by systemic oppression that the question of familial instability was one thing too much? Was it ignorance? Did we lack the cognitive ability to realize the long-term effects of trauma? Was it pride? Did we believe that we could repair our own pain with a stern hand and that we'd be better at it than any outside help could be? Or was it simply out of the question because we were never to see ourselves as weak and to be clear, only White people had those kinds of problems that required professional help. Decades of pretending laid the foundation for the kind of damage that spread like wildfire through generations of bloodlines. It is for that reason, for the need to reveal what has been hidden that this manuscript has been penned. In the safe space of the 21st century, abuse and mental incapacitation is a conversation we are finally ready to have, and the voices in this story, finally like so many others, are equally ready to speak truth to the lies we've told ourselves for far too long. If community means as much as we say it does, then we must take advantage of the times and reroute our paths towards healing. And not one second too soon…

INTRODUCTION

She was a pretty, hazelnut colored baby; creamy textured skin, wide-eyed with a broad smile to match. On one side of her smile was a dimple and on the other was a tiny but noticeable mole. Both seemed to dance when she giggled. She had a head full of wavy, coal colored hair so dense and shiny that the day she was born the pediatric nurses who had not assisted during the delivery and did not know that she had just been birthed by a Negro mother saw her laying in the nursery and assumed that the baby must be of some exotic or mixed descent. There was so much the unsuspecting nurses who cooed over her didn't know. As pretty as she was, she was also the product of incest, and inarguably the worst kind imaginable.

Her mother's name was Charlotta Samuel. She was the oldest of three girls, all of whom were born to a father who loved them in ways he should not have. Charlotta, the first to be given, was the only one to bear the visual proof of her father's wicked lust. She wasn't specifically or deliberately selected to give birth to her father's child; the fact is that her pregnancy was by default really since she, being the oldest, had reached puberty before the other girls. Inevitably Charlotta was the one who carried her unwanted baby in a womb that would be barren after the baby's departure. She and the child created by the incestuous act of a man who assumed he had a right were, therefore, both biological sisters, and simultaneously daughter and mother. And in the duality of the relationship, between them there was nothing but disorder, hurt, self-denial, shame and anger; emotions that Charlotta was so used to, she couldn't remember a time when she didn't feel them.

Grey Samuel was the man who never thought about the damage his inbreeding would cause and no one ever tried to stop him. Theirs was an affair that was never consensual on Charlotta's part and the baby, his baby, would be a haunting reminder of her inability to choose. Permission was never granted because approval would strip such a man of his power over those too weak and too fearful to defend themselves. She was the seed that was damned by the offense from which it was planted; the manifestation of both his demons and Charlotta's numb existence. Grey Samuel was grandfather and father to his eldest daughter's child, impregnated when she was just a child without a voice to object; and Grey Samuel was a pedophile.

Her grandmother, Jorja Sweet, who's first and middle names had always been said as if one, birthed three girls for Grey Samuel. The oldest of which bore her likeness more than the younger two. When her first daughter came into the world, Jorga Sweet thought she'd love her forever. She'd never felt that kind of love for another living thing and she promised to be the best mother she could be. She didn't know that the man she married, who procreated their child, would be the reason her promise to Charlotta would be broken. The child she loved fiercely at first would eventually be the source of her utter despair.

She'd married in the county court house eight months after saying hello, the baby had come six months after the 'I do's," and three months after her arrival, Jorga Sweet's husband turned into a monster. He'd always been a stern man, but the first time he hit her for taking too long to nurse the baby and talking back when he told her so, she knew she'd be fighting him for the rest of life. She was abused into submission and accepted what she could not change; what she did not have the strength enough to walk away from. Jorja Sweet was a shattered woman who couldn't protect herself and wouldn't protect her babies, and a woman who just didn't have enough of herself living inside of herself to be anything other than who he commanded her to be.

The second daughter came two years after Charlotta, and the baby girl came two years after that, both made by him taking Jorga Sweet against her will. Camille and Carmen Samuel – one only fondled, the other also penetrated but not impregnated – were helpless and useless components in Grey Samuels' twisted sport. They were the smallest and most powerless players like pawns in a game of chess in which the winner was always the same. Carmen grew into a woman devout in her faith but still a great pretender who'd mastered the art of illusion, portraying to the watchful eyes of the public a perfect picture for her less than picture-perfect family. Camille became a sexually confused addict and escape artist whose foolish and obnoxious behavior protected the little girl inside of her who only wanted to be loved

.

Charlotta named the bastard child of her father Merci, a befitting name for a girl who would grow into a woman afraid and unsure of whom she was. And she was the result of Grey Samuel's illness; a rancid sickness that seeped into her family's bloodline and grew like an aggressive strand of Cancer until everyone conceded to its defeat over them.

If ever God needed to have mercy on a soul, hers was one for sure. Merci's only asset, or so she had come to accept based on the captivated reaction that people had to her, was a natural and radiant beauty; the kind that transfixed and seduced the souls of most men, putting them in the mind of things far more complex than sex. Hers was the kind of beauty that could at first make other women stop and stand in awe when she entered a room, and then immediately after make her the source of envy and distrust from those very same women who might have otherwise offered her friendship if every man in the room wasn't watching her.

So, for Merci, her beauty was no fortune. It only made her life complicated. It made her too visible in a world where she just did not want to be seen. And since it was solely contingent upon her will she preferred to live like that long-haired, blonde chic on I Dream of Jeanie; enclosed, elusive and almost inaccessible, emerging only when she really felt like it and strictly on her own terms. Those terms were as shallow as the beauty everyone seemed so focused on; purely physical, void of connection and love, without depth, and without the promise of forever.

Many of the girls who grew up envying whom they misjudged Merci to be had no idea that while she was stunning on the outside, Merci felt scarred and ugly on the inside. She was that girl who the other girls stood around in circles and talked about. Remarks like *"She think she cute"* thrown at Merci's back like daggers every time she'd pass them in the hallways of her junior high school; jealous because they had not had the good fortune of being born with Merci's skin color, nor her soft brown eyes and *good hair*, which meant it was naturally long and its soft waves were manageable without being treated by lye relaxers. The beauty mark positioned just so at the very edge of her smile confirmed it; Merci was one of the beautiful people and they were not. Their mistreatment and deliberate disregard bore a deep hole in Merci's soul through which all of her esteem and self-worth fell, and was forever lost in the abyss within.

If only those girls at school would have dared to actually talk to her, get to know her, Merci would have confessed to them that she didn't feel beautiful at all. She was perplexed about and resentful of how she looked, and the isolation made her lonely. Although boys did everything they could to win her attention, she intentionally disregarded them hoping that her female peers would notice her effort to seem insignificant, but they never did. She hated her skin and her eyes and her hair. She just wanted to blend in. She wanted some close girl friends to hang out with, share make-up tips with and discuss the growing pains of being a teenager with. She wanted someone to see beyond her physical attributes and care about who she really was behind the beauty mole.

And at home, Merci's feeling of invisibility only seemed to be more prominent. No one in her family ever looked her directly in her eye, and they hung their heads low in her presence. They never talked to her, but talked over her like she wasn't even there, or at her as if they were always angry with her just because she was there. They were constantly whispering around her, so much so that she wondered what the secret was and why she was the only one not allowed to know. Eventually, Merci gave up, but only after her numerous attempts at being seen had failed.

She brought home excellent grades, sang in the church choir, volunteered to help her grandmother with Sunday dinner, or offered to show her aunts and mother the latest dances trying to form some kind of bridge, some kind of connection between herself and her kinfolk. But still, her grandmother always shooed her out of the kitchen and her aunts always feigned too busy or just uninterested in learning the *prep* or the *cabbage patch*. Merci didn't want to feel like she was crazy but she was convinced that she must be diseased or alien because everyone seemed to avoid her like the plague.

That is, everyone except the numerous flow of potential male suitors and they were no consolation because she was bitter about the beauty that attracted them, convinced that they would never see beyond it. Still Merci let them in because even though the heart may be hardened, the body will still crave the touch of human flesh against its own. She bedded whomever she chose, but her emotions were not for the asking. At least their attention was there, and giving them the pleasure of the physical was all it took to keep them satisfied. It worked out well, because she didn't have anything else to give.

It didn't take long for Merci to realize that she was an outsider everywhere, even in her own family, and with nowhere to fit into, she found a suitable resting place inside of her own tiny shell. But like most nuts, she was only hard on the outside. The flesh inside of her outer covering was tender and could easily be chewed into mush if her protective layer ever failed. So she put all of her efforts into building a strong, absolute and impermeable shield, and she grew comfortably numb there.

Merci's mother, Charlotta, acted most times like Merci wasn't even in the same apartment with her, though most of the dwellings they resided in throughout Merci's childhood were small and cramped. There were no two places in those apartments where the two of them could be and not be more than 100 feet apart. She often wondered how it was even possible to be completely ignored by someone when the ability to always see them was unavoidable.

Merci waited for her mother to be a mother for so long; waited for her to share her own coming of age stories, to help Merci learn to navigate through her own becoming. She waited for Charlotta to warn her about testosterone-driven boys who wanted nothing more than to get her out of her panties. Merci waited for any of the women around her to tell her the secrets of being a woman, the intricacies of proper grooming and hygiene, the correct way to insert a tampon, and what kinds of undergarments are best for wearing under white pants. But it never came and she finally accepted that it would never come, and that she was in this world alone.

And when she turned sixteen, a time when most girls her age were leaning how to drive, cheerleading at the Friday night football games, and venturing out for first times on real first dates, Merci came face to face with her own reality and finally understood that her very existence had been unexpected and unwanted, and by all accounts a sin, or at least a crime. She no longer felt trapped by superficial perceptions, nor did she feel invisible. Her existence had finally been given a face, and it was vile. She was a freak of nature and imagined that if anyone looked at her too closely, they'd be able to see how deformed she really was. So instead of praying to be seen, she worked to become further elusive. Having known nothing but the inside of her shell, she finally came to love it there.

If she could go back in time and talk to those 13 and 14-year-old girls whom she shared the classrooms and cafeteria with in middle school, she'd warn them against pining for the possessions and attributes of others. In the words of her grandmother Jorja Sweet, "Never know how much mess someone else got to deal with to appear so happy. God gave each of us something to be thankful for and each of us a burden to carry," she'd mumble through the puffs of her Virginia Slim.

Except, Merci didn't believe in God because she figured that He'd somehow looked passed her too. He'd played a cruel joke on her because He had decided that hers was a body worth giving a heartbeat to. She had been forced into this perverted fate from the moment her seed was planted in its violated womb, and she was one seed that should have never been allowed to grow. How could God be so cruel if He was supposed to be so merciful? If He was so all-knowing, He must have been aware that Merci would suffer and that she would be a constant reminder to Charlotta of the abuse she'd suffered, and that the pain would always be reflected in the only child Charlotta would ever bear.

Merci often questioned God and expected answers that could have never truly satisfied her inquiries. It was a load she never expected to be relieved of. Where was the mercy in that? Jesus only endured the pain of carrying his cross for a few miles and didn't complain about getting nailed to it and left to die because He knew that His reward was a paradise. Was she supposed to be more of a martyr than Christ Himself? What reward would she ever receive from being the dirty little secret in her family?

It was not bad enough that God had not sterilized the pedophile that simultaneously created and destroyed her life and the lives of every woman who was supposed to teach her how to be a woman, but choosing not to pull the plug on the proof of Grey Samuel's affliction was plain and simple mercilessness.

And something else she knew. It made no sense for those who loved this so-called God to believe in His promise of peace, or in His ability to stop bad people from preying on the unprotected, and defecating on the innocence in this world. No one was more of a devout servant of God, no one sang louder during Sunday morning worship, and no one lifted His name up in praise like her grandmother, Jorja Sweet Samuel. But no one had less to be thankful for.

Jorja Sweet had married Grey Samuel when she was just nineteen years old, he was thirty-one. She was, by all accounts, a child who knew nothing about the harsh ways of the world. She had surrendered herself to marriage believing that she'd share a love like the one her parents shared, alive and unwavering, but she was marrying a man who was dead inside. She and the two generations of women that would follow her died the day she said, "I do".

PART ONE

The beds that are made in our lifetime of days are our own to sleep in. Even when we did not make them, we take them Our souls to keep in

Chapter 1: LEAVING SAVANNAH

Josephine met and ran away with Greyson Samuel when she was 17-years-old; he was nine years her senior. Greyson and his best friend Baker Clemson had opened and ran a juke joint that had been quite lucrative; well, as lucrative as two country niggahs could be in an ass-backwards southern town like Savannah, Georgia in 1935. The Black people in Savannah had nothing else to do but go to the bar and drink hooch, listen to Lil Johnson, Lucille Bogan and Bo Carter sing The Blues, and dance the kind of sweet low down dances that made them forget how poor they were in the midst of the worst economic crisis in America.

One look at the fine car Greyson drove, the tailored pants that fit his buttocks just so and the expensive looking shoes that adorned his feet, and Josephine was ready to go anywhere he wanted to take her. She took in every inch of him with her watchful eye and thought to herself that with a name like Greyson, a name uniquely its own and unheard of in these parts, he must be on his way to being somebody. Josephine liked the way his name sounded rolling off her tongue, and that was before she even knew that she'd be screaming it out in the back seat of that big pretty car. Two weeks of being fucked silly sealed the deal. When he shared his dream with her about getting out of Savannah and going to New York City to open a night club in Harlem, she packed her bags, kissed Savannah and her mother's cheek goodbye, and left.

They traveled all night and into the early morning. It had rained the entire time. If Josephine wasn't so enamored by the man sitting next to her, she might have taken all that rain as an omen. Eight hours in the car made the trip seem less grand to Josephine. By the time they got to the Louisville, Kentucky, it was still raining and she just felt cramped and irritated. One hour and half north of Louisville, and they were coming across a bridge over the Ohio River and headed into Cincinnati, OH.

Josephine looked out the window of the car at the muddy water beneath the bridge and despite its murkiness, she felt a sense of emancipation emulating from its surface. She concentrated on the raindrops hitting the river and her frustration with being in the car seemed to dissipate with every drop that fell. The Ohio River had always been known as the first point of freedom and the entrance to the promise of opportunity in the North, and seeing it for the first time made Josephine know that she would never go any further south than its border ever again. She intended to get to Harlem, get settled in and send for her mother. There wasn't anybody else in Savannah she'd ever need to see.

Greyson looked over at the beautiful brown girl he had spent the last few weeks with and wondered if he had made a mistake by bringing her with him. She was absolutely beautiful. Her skin was perfectly brown and smooth like strong coffee from freshly ground coffee beans with just a touch of sweet milk in it. Her almond shaped eyes seemed to look into a man with a knowing no 17-year-old should have. Her lips were so pouty and well defined on her face that even without lipstick they seemed glossy and inviting like they were blowing kisses with every word she spoke. Besides, she had fallen so hard for him so quickly and had given him her virginity, Greyson felt like he owed her something and the best he could offer was to take her with him on his adventure. He figured if she turned out to be a hassle, he could always send her back to Savannah on the Greyhound.

As they came to the end of the bridge, Greyson decided they should stop for the rest of the night. He had driven without pause since they'd left Savannah, accept to piss, grab a bite to eat, and gas up; his legs were cramped and he was exhausted. Besides, he needed to touch base with Baker, who had made the same drive just three months before, to give his friend an update on his location and to see if Baker had made the final payment to the Jewish guy they had purchased the bar from.

Greyson reached over and stroked Josephine's shoulder, pulling her out of the recesses of her mind, "Hey pretty girl, we're going to stop here and get a room, a sit down meal, and a little rest. I know you sick of being in this car."

Josephine smiled brightly and responded, "A meal and some place to stretch out my body sounds good to me." She leaned over and kissed Greyson's check. "Besides, it's been too long since I've had some of your good love daddy." She moaned the sentiment in the most seductive way she knew how, and Greyson retracted his doubt about having her along for the journey.

Greyson didn't know much about this girl, but she was for sure fine and had some good pussy, and she knew how to make a man feel good. He wondered again how in God's name this woman-child could know these things. She had incredible sex but she didn't have the graces or sophistication of a more experienced woman. He was sure, however, that she could be taught. He'd just have to get her around some mature, classy city women once they got to Harlem and she would lose that country demeanor she had been accustomed to in Savannah.

Greyson pulled off I-75 onto an exit ramp labeled River Road. He drove along the winding, uphill street for about four miles when he saw a run-down motel named after the road it sat on, The River Road Motel. Directly across the street from the River

Road Motel was a restaurant that looked like it was not frequented by local patrons very much at all. Its sign, Mabelle's Good Eating, had several letters with the bulbs burned out and the windows were damn near black from what looked like years of dirt build up and specks of mud water from the Ohio River. But at that point, Greyson didn't care. He just didn't want to drive anymore. He wanted to eat and then lay on his back while Josephine rode up and down on his manhood until he fell asleep from exhaustion.

They ate first then paid for a key to one of the gloomy little rooms at the motel. When Greyson got to the room, he immediately grabbed the phone to call the number Baker had given him before he had left Savannah. The phone just rang. Greyson hung up and figured Baker must be out taking care of business or checking out the scene and the competition on and around Lenox Avenue, the street that would soon house their establishment; rightfully planned to be named the Down Home Juke Joint.

Greyson hung up the phone a little put-off by there being no answer, but the stars in his eyes glowed as if being illuminated by the very lights that would burn the name of his bar every jumping night in the up and coming Negro Mecca in the east. As he thought about the celebrity he intended to acquire on Harlem's bustling scene, Greyson released the telling feeling in his gut and decided to call again in the morning before they got back on the road.

27

Greyson and Josephine spent the day and a good part of the evening hours fucking and talking about the life they were getting ready to have, and then slept until they heard a tremendous clamor outside the motel window at 6:30 a.m. the next morning. By the time they scrambled out of the bed and over to the window, they realized that the commotion was actually alarms of some sort and what seemed like 100 helicopters circling in the sky.

The scream that escaped Greyson's throat sounded like a child's wail after a spanking, and Josephine pushed up to the window to see what could possible make this strong and virile man scream like that. Greyson held onto the frame of the window and looked out. His six-foot frame, broad shoulders and solid torso took up most of the space, blocking Josphine's view. She stood on tiptoe and stretched her five-foot-four body as much as she could and finally settled for poking her head under his arm to see around him and get a better look at the scene outside.

She was horrified at the sight of the river gushing over its banks and the rescue helicopters flying low, just above the water looking for floating bodies, dead or alive. The street they had driven in on had already been covered and the water was rising rapidly.

The good thing was that the River Road Motel, like

all of the buildings that were erected across the road opposite of the rivers bank, sat up high on a sizable hill and then on stilts that made it rise over the road below and out of harm's way when the river flooded. Grey and Josephine had had to park the car and climb what seemed like dozens of steps to get to the front door of the motel's rental office.

The bad thing was that the parking lot of the motel, along with MaBelle's and all the other buildings that sat on the river's bank, was level with the road below. Even if there could have been a road built from the street to the motel, it would have been too steep to have a parking lot on. They stood in that window and watched the Ohio River swell until it covered the top of Greyson's Lincoln Zephyr, and reached more than half way up the dirty windows of MaBelle's, washing them with the muddy water but somehow making them look cleaner than they were when she and Greyson sat there eating the day before. Then she watched Greyson fall back on the bed and cry as if he was being swallowed up too.

In that instance, Josephine briefly thanked God that she had brought her suitcase in with her instead of leaving it in the car and grabbing what she needed for the night out of it like Greyson had suggested. She didn't have a lot of clothes and only two pair of shoes, but she felt sorry for Greyson knowing that all his finely tailored pants that had fit his buttocks so nicely were in that washed-up car. Watching its top disappear, the vehicle didn't seem as grand as it had the first time she saw it. Three days later, when the river retreated back behind its banks and they were able to emerge from the motel room, Greyson ran down those steps at neck-breaking speed and fell on his knees beside what used to be his beautifully colored, expensively upholstered, and finely kept vehicle.

Again, he cried but this time he sobbed uncontrollably. The car was damaged beyond repair. The bright blue paint had faded and was peeling in random spots all over the car. The inside seats and carpeted floors were soaked and layered with mud so heavy you couldn't even tell what color they had been. Greyson didn't care about the muddy seats. He threw the car door open, now squeaky and rusty, and flung himself behind the steering wheel. He stuck the key in the ignition and turned it to the on-position. The drowned car didn't even make a single sound.

Greyson started crying again. Josephine didn't think he'd ever stop. She thought silently to herself that he should be grateful that the damn thing had not floated away. Those old cars were heavy, made of steal. If they had been near an ocean during a flood, the car might have been carried away into its depths, but not the Ohio River. It could flow fast, but didn't have enough width or depth to push a car as big and heavy as this one.

When he finally pulled it back together and let the

tears dry up well enough to be able to see, Greyson returned to the room and tried calling Baker. Again, the phone just rang. Greyson would dial that number at least fifty more times over the next day before he picked the phone up and threw it against the wall of the room.

"That motherfucker!" Greyson screamed the obscenity over and over again until his voice became hoarse. That was how Josephine and Greyson ended up in Cincinnati, Ohio, by being stranded there, and once they made a life there, they couldn't find a reason to leave.

****

There had been no insurance on the car so it wasn't like someone else was going to pay to get it fixed. Besides, it was beyond repair. Greyson had about two thousand dollars in his pocket and Josephine had none. Baker had all the other money Greyson had ever earned and saved. He never found out if Baker bought a bar in Harlem and made it big. He never fulfilled that dream for himself, at least not in Harlem.

At first, Greyson held onto the flimsy hope that this set back was a temporary glitch in the operation and nothing was going to stop him from finding Baker and his money. But after a couple of years and after things had turned around for him in Cincinnati, he stopped hoping to find Baker and his money and made the most of the good fortune he had found.

The businessman in him was all he knew to rely on. Greyson immediately located and surveyed Cincinnati's black neighborhoods and the bars in them. He'd settled on a place called The Village of Lincoln Heights in the Mill Creek Valley, positioned just north of the Cincinnati city limits. It was the first self-governing community north of the Mason-Dixie Line, and an upcoming Black industrial suburb progressively moving towards affluence. The Black people in the more inner-city neighborhoods were poor Black people, and he needed a bar in an area of town whose patrons could afford to pay a little extra for some live entertainment.

Lincoln Heights was affluent in theory because its citizens, all of who were working class people who'd had enough sense to save some money and knew enough to buy some property before the downswing of the economy, said it was. But in reality and for all intent purposes, it was a bottom area of the white northern suburbs of Glendale and Sharonville. The neighborhood sat snugly between Interstate 75 to its east, a railroad track to its west which separated it from the Village of Woodlawn, and the White working-class neighborhood of Lockland to its south. To its credit and Grey's delight, Lincoln Heights was also home to the most patronized juke joint outside of the city called The Peppermint Lounge, and Greyson intended to use his connections to become the entertainment bookie there.

But first things first; with some of the money he had, Greyson moved he and Josephine into a one-bedroom apartment in the Valley Homes, a housing development that was situated at the south entrance of the neighborhood; or exit, depending on which direction you were driving on Anthony Wayne Avenue.

Greyson purchased a sofa, chair, coffee table, lamp and a 13-inch black and white TV for the living room from a man who was moving out of the apartment next door to theirs and heading back down south to take care of an ailing parent. Greyson then purchased a few dishes, pots, pans, and utensils from the thrift store, and turned the phone on too. He needed the phone to conduct his business. He bought some towels, face cloths and other hygiene necessities from the Dollar General and put some groceries in the refrigerator as well.

The only expense that he did not spare, bargain for, or shop thriftily to obtain was for the purchase of a mattress and box spring from Sears Reobuck. He couldn't afford a frame or headboard right away, but figured a mattress would suffice for a short while. It was a bit of a splurge, but he did need a comfortable place to make love to Josephine upon. He didn't understand why, but he was feeling something like love for this almond-eyed, smooth skinned, perfectly brown girl with perfectly round curves. And in truth, he didn't have the heart to send her back to Savannah. But the even bigger truth was that he didn't really want to.

Though modest in its furnishings, the apartment was livable, and Josephine felt safe. She looked at Greyson with the highest esteem while she stood at the kitchen sink washing the dirty dishes from the first of many meals they'd share in their new home. And he played the part for her of the valiant knight coming to her rescue. He had a plan, which was what Josephine was getting used to about him. She knew that the Valley Homes was only going to be a temporary residence, but something about the way he made her feel made her believe that their relationship was going to be anything but temporary.

The only word she could think of to describe the swimming feeling in her stomach when he held her was fluid. He'd given definitive shape to that liquid feeling when he promised her, and himself, that in less than six months he'd have a new car and in a couple of years he would be able to save enough money to buy a house; show her the life he was used to living.

The new houses going up every which way in Lincoln Heights weren't huge, but they had yards with enough room for children to play and a small garden. They had driveways and garages, and dining rooms. They were two and three bedroom modernly designed homes with brick, not wooden structures.

And some even had what the northerners called a half bathroom for guests with only a toilet and a basin, in addition to the whole bathroom that included a bathtub. Greyson was intent on having one of them to call his own. And Josephine was more than content to let her man take care of business, and take care of her.

That first night in the apartment felt oddly familiar to Josephine, as if this was exactly what she'd always imagined for her life. She finished cleaning up the kitchen, and decided to take a bath. It was the one thing she couldn't wait to do since the moment she walked into the apartment. In Savannah, her mother's house did not have a porcelain tub that was long enough to stretch her legs all the way out in front of her, instead there was only the round tin washtub that had also been used to wash clothes in. She intended to take full advantage of the spacious tub and the relaxation.

So eager to get out of the kitchen and into her bathroom paradise, Josephine planted a soft, brief kiss of Greyson's forehead as she rushed past him up the stairs to second level of their home, and left him sitting on the sofa with a little black phone book in one hand and the phone receiver cradled on his shoulder, calling up his old friends from the Chittlin Circuit to cash in on some of the favors he was owed. So engrossed in getting his plan into motion, Greyson didn't even look up but was momentarily grateful that Josephine understood that now was not the time to distract him with more than a passing gesture of affection.

Back in Savannah, Greyson had been able to get his juke joint on the Chittlin Circuit. Negro musicians were just niggahs who could sing back then, not worthy of being visible in the mainstream, and they damn sure weren't invited to grace the stages of places like Carnegie Hall or the dance floors in the legendary Roseland Ballroom, even though they were far more talented than their White counterparts. This underground circuit of popular joints in predominantly Negro towns like Harlem, Baltimore, and yes, Savannah, GA, gave a voice to a generation of Negro entertainers whose sounds and profits were being stolen by the larger, more powerful record industry that had not been quite ready to see Black people on their album covers, even when sometimes it would be their voices overlaying the tracks.

But there were Negro-owned bars all throughout the south and along the eastern border, even a few scattered throughout the Midwest, south from St. Louis and as far north as Chicago and Detroit, that opened their doors and the promise of their patrons to these artists. Wherever there were Negro folks living and loving through poverty and struggle, there was a home for The Blues. The artists on the Chitlin Circuit had a prime and most sought after spotlight of guaranteed bookings on the regular schedule of entertainers who came and went, on and off those stages every night.

The regularity of the steady work, the organized and centralized contracting of the gigs, and the promotions of sometimes three-night and sometimes four-night repeatedly ran shows is what gave birth to the idea that they had created a circuit of sorts. Those hard singing, hip grinding men and women belted out the kind of down-home lyrics that the Negro community lived for; songs that told their stories and made them forget how desolate the narratives were. On the circuit, the artists were welcomed and paid, and so they found peace with their Chittlin Circuit fame, and left stages on fire in those smoke-filled, dance-sweaty bars located in the urban parts of those cities already known for their nightlife. Even though Lincoln Heights was not yet known for its night-life, if Greyson Samuel had anything to do with it, its popularity would soon be on the rise. Hell, even suburban niggahs with a little bit of money still wanted to party hard and he intended to make sure they could. The Peppermint Lounge had enough notoriety to be propelled to the next level.

The next afternoon when the Peppermint Lounge opened its doors for a usually long day of business, Greyson was crossing its threshold close on the heels of its owner, Leroy Pepper, a sawed-off, chubby man with a red face and a receding hairline. Rumored to be half-Indian, Peppers complexion was that of sawdust. But Josephine had never known of any Indians to be as fat as him, so she assumed that he was really just some half-bred Negro boy whose Caucasian ancestry was closer in his bloodline than the darker skinned Negroes.

Pepper, as he was commonly known by the regulars who frequented the dance floor, the booths and the barstools of the lounge, wobbled through the front door of his bar that humid summer morning with Greyson following hastily behind, but busied himself turning on the three fans spread out an equal distance from one another around the elaborately designed bar before he even acknowledged that Greyson was standing there. Greyson, who did not really need Pepper's acknowledgement or permission to get comfortable, moved to occupy the corner seat at the bar located next to the first fan that Pepper had operated.

By the time Pepper placed his eyes, set deep in pudgy sockets and behind heavy, lazy lids, on Greyson, he was instantly aware that he was there for business. Greyson pitched his proposal and Leroy ate it up like it was a five course meal and he was the king for which the feast had been prepared. Pepper made a decent profit at the bar, but the idea of the amount of money he could make with live entertainment from the still well-known underground singers this Mr. Samuel was talking about bringing in made plump beads of greedy sweat run like water down Pepper's rotund little face.

For 10 years, Greyson brought singer after singer to the Peppermint Lounge. He negotiated all the money and took his cut off the top. Being in the "entertainment" business was hard work indeed, but its privileges were abundant. He was well respected in the neighborhood and had been given favor in the most important Negro circles in the city. There were plenty of women at his disposal, though he always came home to Josephine, even after she'd had their son, and had stopped going with him to the lounge at nights.

He made her an honest woman and married her soon after the boy had been born. They named him Grey, though Josephine wanted him to be a junior with his father's exact name, Greyson felt that it was important for children to have their own identities. The money was good, the living was good. Josephine got as much notoriety as Greyson and she enjoyed being the focus of attention when she'd walk the neighborhood pushing her precious baby boy in his stroller. And like Greyson promised, he'd purchased, with cash, and moved them into a modest but well-built home on Fulton Avenue, a dead-end street on the west side of the neighborhood furthest from the east-lying highway.

But after just a decade in Cincinnati, the circuit was seeing its last days. By 1950, no one really cared to listen to those gritty blues that resounded in a hoarse, almost growling timbre anymore. Negro music was changing. It was, on one hand, mellowing out and finding a soulful rhythm that would give birth to R&B and would eventually usher in the soul era. Instead of love lost and hard times, folks started writing songs about love found and good days coming. And on the other hand, some Negroes had crossed over into this new craze called Rock and Roll, a genre eventually replicated by Little Richard, international British bands and the likes of Elvis Presley.

Many of the people who had been really popular on the circuit had gotten mainstream deals and were too busy trying to entertain a crossover audience to make time for places like The Peppermint anymore. And the ones who never quite reached industry celebrity could no longer afford to chase their dreams. The gigs weren't paying like they used to, or maybe it was inflation that had lowered its heavy cross on the population. But traveling to get to gigs hundreds of miles away cost more than they could earn when they got there. Live entertainment was being replaced by disc jockeys that spun vinyl albums of recorded soul artists like Brook Benton and Sam Cooke.

When the good times ended, so did Greyson's interest in being in Cincinnati. He tried to get up every morning and pretend like putting on steal-toe boots to go to work in the mills and factories was enough for him. But it wasn't in Greyson to be regular, nor was he used to working for someone else. Greyson woke up one morning, and realizing that he had no business to tend to, decided that he'd reached the end of his rope. He told Josephine that he was going to take a vacation by himself for a couple of weeks, to get his head cleared out.

He left and never came back, but had left the bank account open with a little over $5000 dollars in it and a note for Josephine explaining that he needed to find a new dream. The note had been stuck to the box of Christmas ornaments and decorations in the garage. It was just a week before Thanksgiving when he left, so he knew that Josephine would soon be pulling that box out in another two weeks, as it was her custom to decorate for Christmas one week after Thanksgiving.

Like clockwork, she did just that, as soon as the leftover turkey had been made into hash and turkey salad. When she found the note, she forgot all about the Christmas decorating. She retreated to her bedroom, got into the bed and up under the cover, and cried herself into a fitful slumber that was interrupted only by her 5-year-old son tugging on her hair and whining about being hungry.

The months immediately following Greyson's departure had just about killed Josephine, but she soon rebounded when she realized that the five thousand dollars had dwindled quickly from her lack of budgeting sense. The fairytale life she had known was over. If she was going to manage, she needed a plan because an instant miracle was most likely not on the way.

Chapter 2: BEHIND CLOSED DOORS

Grey Samuel was raised in the kind of household with a lot of closed doors; doors that held behind them his mother's dark and nasty secrets. For most of his adolescent and teenage years, the rooms behind all those closed doors smelled like old sex and stale cigarette smoke, left behind by the patrons who spent a couple of hours at a time in them.

He hated those rooms and those damn closed doors. Their house, the house his father had purchased with his hard earned money and that Grey never saw as belonging to anyone else but his father, once saw the constant flow of his father's business constituents, and later, those of his mother's. Grey preferred the open space of the back porch. It was screened in but spacious, with just enough furniture to make it comfortable. And there he could not hear the wail of the bedsprings being overworked by the bodies that bounced around on them. From that back porch he could not hear the lewd moans of his friends' fathers being pleasured by his mother. There on the back porch, separated by the brick walls of the house, Grey hid from the siren's song of the bedsprings deep in the fading hours of the night.

His mother, Josephine Samuel, was a whore; the whore of the neighborhood and she took care of her family from the money she made on her back. And it was no secret to anyone. In fact, she was a legend of sorts. She was the only whore that anyone around those parts had ever known who'd run her business on her own terms and without a pimp. And she did so right out of the house she had once lived in with her husband, Greyson Samuel, the same house he walked out of and never came back, and the same house she now lived in with her only son, his only son Grey.

She was no streetwalker either. Josephine worked seven hours a day, like her business was a legitimate one, from 11 p.m. to 6 a.m., Tuesday to Saturday, and every man who visited her knew better than to stop by outside of those hours or without an appointment. That's right, they called ahead. And just like any legal business, they spoke with an assistant who scheduled them for their rendezvous.

Josephine grew to hate Greyson Samuel with the same fixation that she had at first learned to love him. She blamed him and his sudden and untimely departure for forcing her into such a lowly career. As far as she was concerned, the only good thing that he had given her that turned out to be permanent was the son she partially named after him and whom she loved so much she sold her body for a living to take care of. She had no other skill. She was too young when Greyson had taken her away from her home and her family in Savannah, Georgia, to learn to do anything else but fuck her man and keep him happy at home. So it was a natural progression for her to ascertain that her sex was her best asset.

Josephine had determined, even before the very first time she recruited her first client, that a pimp would not be required. If she was going to be a whore, she was going to keep every cent she sacrificed the man-trap between her legs for to herself. She had never worked a nine to five and had depended on a man, one man, all of her adult life to make sure she had what she needed; for absolutely everything, from money to spend at the Pogues Department Store downtown, to transportation where she needed to go, to a roof over her head, to the food she cooked and ate every day. Every necessity of her life was given to her, so nothing in her life had ever been earned on her own. If she was going to sell her body, it was going to be a self-earning and self-benefiting endeavor.

And she knew nothing about the finances when Greyson Samuel up and walked away from his wife and his child. It took weeks before Josephine stopped standing at her window for hours a day with a cup of coffee in one hand and a cigarette in the other, waiting on him to walk back up the front steps and through the door. But she did finally close the curtain until the edges of each panel overlapped, shutting all outside light out, and she never opened or allowed anyone else to open those curtains on the front of the house again. Never mind that the best sunlight came in through the picture window, which took up the majority of the street-facing wall of the living room. And never mind how dark and stuffy it made the house feel, all closed up and shut off from natural light. Didn't she know that children, like flowers, need sunlight to grow?

Eventually, she accepted Greyson's abandonment and confident that he wasn't ever coming back, Josephine declared him dead and went about figuring out how to get the money from the life insurance policy she remembered that Greyson had once told her about. It was the only thing he had shared with her about his business. She retrieved the policy from the place Greyson had shown her it would be, read it over and discovered that she needed a death certificate to prove that Greyson was dead. She asked the nephew of a neighbor, whom the entire neighborhood knew was into criminal activity, how she could get one and how much it would cost. He made the arrangements and delivered the product three days later. Josephine paid the criminal and made the call to the insurance agent.

Josephine didn't have a clue what the insurance man was saying to her about policies and payouts. When he was done rambling, it sounded like she was going to have just enough to pay federal and state taxes that she did not know her technically dead husband had not paid, the property taxes owed on the house for that year, and maybe have a penny or two left over. She had a child's mouth to feed, not to mention her own, utility bills to pay and she soon found out, a car to finish paying for too; a car that Greyson had told her was paid off when he was still high-rolling from the profits of the lounge.

How the hell did he think she was going to do all of that with the life insurance money from the measly ass policy and the money he'd left in the bank? How was she supposed to survive without the only person she'd ever needed to take care of her and her baby boy? How could Greyson be so selfish? Those days of not being in control of her own life were over the moment she realized that he was gone and wasn't ever coming back. She would make her own money and never again be unaware of where every cent of her money was and how it was being spent.

She had not set out to be a prostitute. It wasn't like it was her dream job. She had tried cleaning house for the rich white folks in Indian Hills and Glendale, which was one of the few shitty dream jobs a 27-year-old Colored girl with no real job skills and no employment history could get in the early 50's; that, or working in a factory, standing on a concrete floor for eight or ten hours a day on an assembly line. She thought that both alternatives would be as back-breaking, but with less profit as the profession she had chosen. Besides, having never seen a day of manual labor in her life, her dainty hands with the perfectly manicured and polished nails and her well maintained body were in no way equipped for the kind of toil required by those jobs. She, like her vanished husband, was accustomed to the good life.

It had been just over ten years earlier when Greyson, finding himself and his new girlfriend stuck in a city he had no knowledge of, set a plan in motion, but with him gone and Josephine left to fend alone, it seemed like a lifetime ago. Greyson surely had not included Josephine in or consulted with her about any business decision he'd ever made. He managed all the money, she never saw it coming or going. She got an allowance and all she cared to know was that she could spend as she pleased. But now, by herself and with a lifestyle to maintain, Josephine shifted into action, making a plan of her own for the very first time in her life.

By the way she handled her business it became surprisingly apparent to Josephine that she had gotten more from Greyson Samuel than her sweet-faced baby boy after all. She had been learning the operations of a business without even being cognizant that she was absorbing the goings on. All along, it appeared as if she was just present, but never aware; just the good and subservient housewife, doting lover and attentive mother she was expected to be. She had supported Greyson and had earned her keep by being his pretty young thing; a well-stacked showpiece whose job consisted of taking care of home, of their son, and of his needs.

But in spite of having lived as a trophy, Josephine found what to her seemed to be a reasonable way to become the boss. She ran her business in the same tightly managed manner that her husband had run his. There was an assistant who took the appointments, confirmed the nature of the services that were to be rendered that evening, established what monies would be paid, and greeted the clients when they arrived. She'd lead them to their din of iniquity, offering them libation once they were settled in and waiting for Josephine's entrance. She was something to wait for. Her exotic beauty, her round and firm breasts that sat up so high they appeared to be reaching for her chin , and her warm and wet vagina were all the neighborhood fathers and husbands could talk about; trading fabricated stories on the factory floors and barber shops.

Josephine had been in business for only three months when she realized that she just did not have enough time in the day to run a business, be a mother to her six-year-old, and keep house. Her assistant's name was Roxanne Drummond and she was nineteen-years-old when she first started working for Josephine. Grey was only six-years-old, but he remembers when Roxanne had first become a live-in assistant and maid for his mother. He knows he was six because he was in the first grade and it was exactly four seasons after his father had left. At first, Roxanne's only duties were to perform basic secretarial tasks for the business, but later she would be promoted to keeping the house clean, the clothes washed, and the meals served on time.

After two years in the business and a gradual progression in their relationship, from maid to matron, from employer to mentor, and from associate to confidant, Roxanne's duties were further increased. In the 50's, she was just live in help, but today she'd be called an executive personal assistant. It had only cost Josephine room and board, and an offer of decent weekly wages to gain a daughter of sorts and Josephine had grown to trust her.

As an added duty, Roxanne began collecting the money from the patrons at the end of their services, and routinely depositing the day's earnings in the safe that Josephine kept on lock in the back of her bedroom closet. As a part of her initial chores, she'd then change the linens after each client left while Josephine readied herself for the next customer to arrive. She was Josephine's right hand, but one thing she was not was a nanny. Josephine was adamant about that. Roxanne was there to help her run her business, and maintain the daily functions of her home, freeing up time for Josephine to mother her only and adored son.

Josephine spent time with Grey every day. Her last customer would be out of the house by 6:00 a.m. every morning. She'd nap for an hour after the last men would leave her bed, then she'd be up, showered and in Grey's room bending down to kiss his face with the same lips that had whispered practiced sighs in the dark and explored horny and hard body parts just hours before. In the shadows of the night and behind her closed door, she was every temptress that she was called on to be, but in the light of day she was just Grey's mother.

Every morning Josephine got Grey dressed for

school while Roxanne cooked his breakfast. Josephine would then walk Grey to the bus stop and stay with him until the bus came. Meanwhile back at the house, Roxanne busied herself gathering lacey undergarments and bedding from the dirty clothes hamper for the wash, and putting away the props, lotions and whatever other tricks of the trade Josephine had engaged her clients with. Roxanne would already have a load of the cum stained lingerie and bed sheets in the washer and have Josephine's bed redressed with clean sheets by the time she got back from taking Grey to the bus stop. Roxanne would also have the money from the night's business counted and if it were Friday, she'd count out her week's pay before the daily deposit was made. Accounts of the earnings were reported to Josephine while she ate her breakfast.

During the rest of the day while Josephine slept, Roxanne busied herself with running errands to the grocery store, the dry cleaners, and whatever other chores needed to be done around the house, and finding time for her own personal life when she could. She began to take the night's appointments by mid-afternoon from the tricks that would begin to show up at the door later that evening in a steady stream. But Josephine would be up by 3:30 every afternoon to meet Grey at the bus stop when he returned from school.

By the time Josephine and Grey would make it back from the bus stop, Roxanne would have dinner started and a small snack prepared for mother and son to enjoy while Josephine helped Grey with his homework. All three would sit for dinner and then enjoy some quality time together listening to 45s on the turntable and dancing about in the living room, or watching a family oriented television program, doing puzzles, or coloring in one of Grey's many coloring books. And when the weather was nice, not too hot and muggy like Midwest summers could be and not too blistery like winters always got, the three of the them would just hang out in the yard so that Grey could run and jump like growing boys are supposed to do while the ladies tended to the garden or reclined on the covered porch drinking lemonade and talking business.

At 8:00 p.m. every evening, like clockwork, exactly three hours before the proverbial punching of the clock, Josephine would get Grey ready for bed, bathe him and read him a bedtime story. By 9, Grey would be tucked away and sound asleep, and she could begin getting ready for "work", which consisted of a hot bubble bath, taking care of any necessary grooming, smoking a joint, having two glasses of Cabernet, and listening to Nina Simone sing her into a lulled state of mind.

Also to her mothering credit, Josephine took Grey to church every single Sunday. She worked five days a week, took two days for herself, and though Saturdays were her busiest day of the week, she and Grey never missed church and managed to make it every week for 9:00 am Sunday school. She would be bone tired most Sunday mornings but stayed awake after her last trick was turned to baptize herself in lavender and lemongrass infused bath water that she laid in with closed lids meditating and praying away the night's discretions. She'd get herself dressed before awaking her little lion to get him ready, humming *Precious Lord* the entire time. They'd be walking out the whore house on their way to the holy house by 8:30 a.m.

For Josephine, it was the most important thing she could do for the soul of her son. She had been raised in church, never missed a Sunday in Savannah on the second pew with her mother, and she truly believed in God. She'd stopped going to church when Greyson brought her to the north, but made her way back to the flock just months after he'd left. She knew that her profession was not one that her neighbors and her heavenly father smiled upon, but those few hours in God's house each week with her child made Josephine feel redeemed.

She knew that prostitution was not the kind of job that would ever be honored, but she'd done it with such decisiveness and direction, no one could ever say she was a victim. She was silently admired by repressed housewives who'd wished they had the guts to do what she did instead of falling apart like most of them would have done if they'd been abandoned. Josephine didn't care who felt what, it was just business for her, no different than the jobs they dragged their bodies to everyday. She didn't seek their approval and since she was grown and her mother had long been gone, she saw no need to consider the opinion of women who thought she needed more rearing.

Josephine talked to God directly and privately from the altar every Sunday, and she believed He understood, and that she would not be condemned. Hell, Jesus himself allowed a whore to wash his feet and for her humbled servitude, He forgave her of her discretions. If Mary Magdalene could be forgiven, so could she. Whatever judgment she stood to receive, Josephine believed that hell would not be her eternal resting place. Her soul was clean, even if her body was a little soiled.

One Sunday morning as Josephine and little Grey ascended the dozen or so steps that led to the doors of the church where she received her weekly cleansing, she was approached by Ida Franklin's bourgeoisie ass. She pushed her ample bosom up to Josephine and had the nerve to ask her how she could show her face in the house of the Lord. Josephine looked right into Ida's eyes, discreetly grabbed her arm for affect, leaned in close enough to kiss Ida on her ear, and through tightly clenched teeth told Ida to kiss her ass in a whisper so low that Grey, who stood right next to her, could not hear. Josephine squeezed Ida's arm a little harder and spit words that must have felt like fire in her ears.

"Listen you bitch, my business with God ain't no business of yours. His mercy reaches everyone, no matter how low on earth they are. He might even have mercy on your husband. Bill likes for me to lick that mole on the right side of his navel just before I climb on top of him." Grey had no idea what his mother had said to Ms. Ida, but the tears that welled up in her eyes told him that Josephine had cut her deeply.

Josephine thought she'd had every base covered. And everything was copasetic until Grey turned 12-years-old and became more aware of what his mother did for a living; all his friends knew too. He had to face them every day knowing that they had wet dreams inspired by his mother and by the time they were 14-year-old teenagers with raging hormones racing fiercely towards manhood, they'd grown comfortable with verbalizing their horny desires about Josephine.

Grey always wondered what the hell his mother was thinking about. She was "servicing" his friend's fathers and uncles and thought his friends weren't going to ride him about it, like their father's rode her night in and night out. They never let up about how good the men-folk in the neighborhood said his mother's pussy was, and how they wished they were old enough to get it too. But everyone knew Josephine had rules, and one of those rules was that you had to be an adult to fuck her. You had to be at least 25 years of age to be invited to her party. And

Josephine's rules were respected, even though in general, she was not. Grey would laugh off their jiving and in retaliation would jokingly call their mothers dirty names, even though they were not.

Grey seldom hung out in his friend's homes or played in their yards because their mothers made him feel uncomfortable with their stares of contempt, as if it were his fault that his mother was fucking their husbands. The sins of the mother were being visited on the son, and he inwardly hated them all; the boys on the block who called him a friend but openly discussed different positions they'd fuck his mother in, the men who salivated over her body at night and treated her like she was invisible when they saw her in public during the daytime, and the cowardly wives who couldn't please their husbands enough to keep them at home and out of his mother's bed.

He secretly hated his father too, though outwardly he defended Grey's memory. Whenever his friend's ribbing would include anything that questioned his father's manhood in any way for marrying a prostitute, he'd bark back with made-up stories about overhearing his mother and Roxanne discussing one of their father's impotence or small dick. Still, if it wasn't for his father's leaving, Grey would have been able to live a typical teenage boy's life rather than this imposed disgrace and unwarranted blame he was stuck with. He often fantasized about his father coming back, unexpectedly, finding his mother under some man in the bedroom they'd shared and whipping her clear until she passed out. Grey vowed at an early age that no woman would ever be out of his control when in his watch.

While his deepest disdain should have been for his mother, Grey had a love/hate relationship with Josephine. Grey knew that she loved him. She doted over him even when he got too old for her to coddle. She kept the business as far away from him as she could, and she walked the streets of Lincoln Heights like she dared anyone to look at her as if she didn't have a right to be there. These things he understood that Josephine did as a mother to compensate for who she'd chosen to be as a woman, but he hated that she used him as an excuse to fuck for money. He hated that she acted like their life was normal; she'd never even acknowledged directly to Grey that she was a whore, and he never told her that he knew. He protected his mother as much as she tried to protect him and they lived in that fantasy not saying what the other knew; trying to do what each of them thought was best for one another and themselves.

Still no one could deny that Josephine had taken control of her own life and made sure that her son did not miss a beat in the void left by a once providing husband and father; that was all that had ever mattered to Josephine. Grey came to discern that women could be both treacherous and sweet, and if there is no man in her life to make rules and insist that they were obeyed she'd be unable to control herself. He couldn't wait to reach the legal age that would allow him to leave this house, that he could not recall was ever a home, and start his own life with his own rules.

When Grey turned sixteen, Josephine fell ill with some kind of woman's disease he could never recall the name of. The closed up room of his mother that once held the musky smell of discretion began to smell like the slow walk of death, even stronger than the linger of the stale sex and cigarettes. Josephine hadn't died, at least not physically or right away, but she had retired from "the business" and resolved herself to collecting welfare from the government for the rest of her life. And for her side gig (because the skill to hustle had become the platelets in her blood), she bootlegged pints of liquor, cigarettes and marriage counseling to the men in the neighborhood who used to pay for her other skills and whose wives were painfully aware of the transgressions their husbands had committed with her. Even though she was no longer needed to help Josephine run her "business", Josephine kept Roxanne around to help clean house and cook, since these chores had become increasingly difficult for her ailing body to handle.

Grey had stayed with his mother until the day she died. He was turning eighteen the year he committed Josephine's body to the ground. With the dirt from the cemetery still fresh on his shoes, he returned to his childhood house, fired Roxanne, packed up his mother's things, and sat them out for the Goodwill van to retrieve on its weekly rounds. He stuck a for-sale sign in the yard that very night and it was only a matter of weeks before he had a buyer. Grey felt no guilt profiting from the sale of his father's home and his mother's belongings. The only feeling he had was freedom.

With the money that he felt was the least his parent owed him, he got on a Greyhound headed for Oakland, California, with no clear plan in mind, but with no intent to ever return to Lincoln Heights. It didn't matter to Grey that he had never been more than fifty miles outside the boundaries of his neighborhood, nor that he'd know no one in California when he got there. He just knew it was as far away from his childhood as he could get without leaving America, and not knowing anyone meant not being known. Grey took with him a driven intent to define and enforce his own rules in any relationship he encountered especially where the fairer gender was concerned. His luggage held clothes and toiletries, but what he carried was a deep-seated disgust and distrust for women.

But Grey returned to Cincinnati some short-lived ten years later, tired of the influx of Mexicans to the Oakland area and the lack of what he considered suitable women to lock down. The women in Oakland were too citified so Grey fled the west coast for the Midwest home with girls who had been raised to seek a husband to take care of them. But upon his return, Grey touched down to find that his past had been erased. Lincoln Heights didn't look at all like it had before he'd left. The neighborhood had become worn down. The Valley Homes no longer looked like a newly designed housing development. Instead, they just looked like the projects.

The small but neat homes had been abandoned while he was away. The first Black inhabitants had started renting or selling their home and had crossed the tracks and moved one neighborhood over to the Township of Woodlawn where the lawns and homes were a little bit bigger, but barely a mile distance from the seedy element that had taken over Lincoln Heights. Their first homes had grown too small for their growing families and for their pockets. Affirmative action had produced financial progress for those first Black inhabitants of Lincoln Heights, allowing them to relocate their suburban, middle-class lifestyles into Woodlawn, pushing the White middle class who had previously resided there further into the northern parts of the city.

By the time the exodus was coming to an end, the streets of Lincoln Heights had become overrun by a group of Black folks who had economically separated themselves from the welfare recipient class that seemed destined to dwell in the West End, Millville, English Woods and Avondale forever. The second generation of inhabitants had moved on up but were still operating in inner city ways, and had swiftly managed to turn the first neighborhood in the whole state to be settled by Black people into a seedy place.

These new Lincoln Height residents were a lower working-class of people whose jobs weren't as prestigious as the families who had abandoned the neighborhood they now occupied, but they had stayed on them long enough to finally scrape together the money they needed to move out of their inner city to the suburban ghetto. They rented, not owned the homes they resided in, lived check to check, had meager or no savings to speak of, and didn't have much to show for their labor, but were generally decent people whose expectations of life had inevitably been diminished by their urban upbringing. People can only be a reflection of what lives in them despite their well-meaning attempt at escape.

This socioeconomic class of people had brought the ghetto with them and sat it down smack in the middle of Grey's once clean and respected neighborhood. The corners that used to be inhabited by markets and fruit stands were overran by liquor stores and car washes, or maybe the occasional pick-up truck being driven by a less than well-kept man selling watermelons off the back. Grey remembered the time when there was only one adult nighttime hangout in Lincoln Heights and it was The Peppermint Lounge. Now there were bars and after hours joints in almost every block of the neighborhood. The only thing that was sordid in his neighborhood back when he was a youth was his mother. Seeing what had become of Lincoln Heights upon his return, Grey sorely thought to himself that Josephine would have finally fit in.

Grey thought it was sad to see. It was, after all, the eve of the 1970's, a revolution had occurred and Black people were mobilizing and being proud to be Black all over the country. But the only change that had managed to happen to Lincoln Heights was its decline. Grey was shocked, it did not seem to him possible that such a change could have occurred in the near decade he'd lived in California. Finding nothing there to go back to, Grey decided to head downtown to where he was told he could find the YMCA to rent a room. He took a third shift job as a janitor at the General Hospital, just up the Vine Street hill and off MLK Avenue, and because he possessed the charm of his father, the hustle of his mother and the business savvy of both, he worked his way up to shift manager in a matter of months. That's where he saw, met and pursued Jorja Sweet.

She came crashing into the Emergency Room one cold and icy winter night, frantically trailing behind two gurneys with a middle-aged couple occupying one bed each. Both were unconscious, with blood spilling out from every orifice of their bodies. Whatever clothing they were wearing had been cut off by the paramedics with no regard to the cost or the attachment the people may have had to them. Shreds of the clothing could be seen laying in pieces under their mangled bodies.

The beautiful, bronzed colored girl who had come in with the couple was hysterical; just a complete and utter wreck. Not only were her tears coming down in wave after wave of uncontrollable downpours, but her hair was scattered atop her head like she had been in a massive windstorm. There were fragments of glass visibly spread throughout its strands. Her makeup had been smeared so badly that she looked like a clown who had gone swimming in full face. Trickles of liquefied paint were floating down her face and sliding right off her chin in spots that stained her clothing.

And Grey remembered that she wore a pretty teal colored dress that fit like skin from the low cut neckline to the knee, then ended in a single ruffle that hung slightly below. She was shaped perfectly and was making that dress talk with every hurried and manic step she took. Through her disheveled appearance, he could tell that she was a pretty girl. But it wasn't her physical beauty that had Grey held in rapture, she looked so entirely in need of someone to put her back together.

At the door beyond the receiving area, she was stopped by the nurses from entering the trauma unit of the ER along with the wheeled beds that carried her parent's bodies through its double doors, and was led to the receptionist's desk by a nurse who instructed Jorga Sweet to let the doctor's do their jobs and promised that the lead doctor would come and talk to her as soon as he had a prognosis of her parent's condition. While the uninterested medical aid pressed her for insurance information and medically vital information about her parents, Grey decided he was going to offer his assistance, instinctively knowing that Jorga Sweet would accept it.

He first dipped into a nearby restroom, grabbed a hand full of paper towels and wet them with just enough water to wipe her pretty face clean. Grey then went to the vending machine at the other end of the hall and got two cups of coffee. Not knowing if the stranger liked it with crème and sugar or even if she liked it at all, he grabbed a handful of packets from the nurse's station and made his way back to the booth where she sat blindly answering questions. He placed one cup of the coffee he had purchased onto the desk in front of her and pushed it within her reach. He pushed open the fingers of her shaking hand that lay on the desk and placed the makeshift face cloth between them. Then he walked away to go on with his cleaning while sipping on the other cup of java.

When his shift was coming to an end just a few hours later, he knew she'd still be hanging around looking for him to thank him for the coffee and for his kindness. She just looked polite that way. The two of them sat in the lobby of the ER talking into the late hours of the morning. Grey learned that her name was Jorja Sweet, she was an only child, her parents were childhood sweethearts, and she and her parents had been in a car accident that night.

They were driving home from the church's annual Pastor's Appreciation banquet when a truck lost its traction to the road and smashed head on into them, sending their car careening through the guardrail and down a thirty-foot embankment. She had traveled all the way to the bottom with the car, strapped into the back seat. She was tossed around and pounded, disoriented and in some pain by the time the car came to a stop. Her father, who had been driving and not wearing his seatbelt because he never did, had been thrown from the car and had traveled down the embankment without the protection of the car's metal surrounding him. And her mother, who sat in the passenger's seat and had been buckled in, suffered fatal head damage anyway.

In the short time that it took Jorja Sweet to tell him far more about herself than she should have ever told a stranger who'd only offered her coffee and paper towels so far, Grey was able to size her up completely. She was a sweet girl just like her name suggested, who excelled in everything because she was expected to. She was her parents little darling and he could tell. She was smart, but sheltered and naïve. She was a good girl of sorts, but shaped like a woman whom he could enjoy the physical pleasures of while teaching. And now, having watched her mother and father die that night, she was heartbroken and alone. And Grey knew exactly what lonely and broken women like her needed to be healed.

CHAPTER 3: SWEET JORJA ON MY MIND

All the ladies at Greater Good Baptist Church thought that Jorja Sweet was an overzealous do-gooder who volunteered for almost every special events committee, served on the usher board, the Pastor's aid board, taught Sunday School, sang in the choir, directed the youth choir and spent too much time trying to out-do everybody else.

But Jorja Sweet knew and lived what they did not. The Lord's house was the only other house besides her own where she was allowed to be for any significant amount of time without having to suffer the untrusting questions of her husband or feel the sting of his hand across her face for making him suspicious, angry, irritated or any other change of mood he experienced. The gossiping women had no idea that church was truly her only refuge and more than just the reflection of the lyrics in the songs they sang from the choir stand each week. So on Sundays, she and her girls were the first to arrive for Sunday school and were always the last to leave the evening service, usually walking out with Brother Hollister, the trustee who was responsible for locking up.

Every other day of the week was like solitary confinement for Jorja Sweet. Her husband believed that all women needed to be controlled by a stern and unyielding hand, or else they'd forget how to be ladies. Monday through Saturday, Jorja Sweet was prevented from venturing further than her front or back yards, and when she did have somewhere to go she couldn't be gone for longer than an hour, which according to Grey Samuel, was more than enough time to run errands for the household. She had exactly 60 minutes to do whatever she needed to leave the house to do; pick the girls up from school, or go to the grocery store, or to the drycleaners, to the bank, or to the post office. Luckily, she was skilled at doing her own hair because the time it would have taken to get beautified in a salon would not have been permitted.

The women who shared their place of worship with her every Sunday could not reconcile the child they knew with the estranged woman they had come to know. Jorja Sweet couldn't say that she didn't understand how she had developed a reputation for becoming a snob. She'd been a member of Greater Good and of the neighborhood for all of her life and they had known her since she entered this world, had watched her grow up, and had helped to bury her parents. Her now elusive behavior, isolation, and all around less than inviting presence disappointed them. It looked like she had changed when she married Grey Samuel, and they knew it was not something her mother or father would have approved of.

Grey dressed Jorja Sweet and his girls up in fine clothes like they were plastic Barbie dolls; elaborate exterior coverings meant to hide the worn and deteriorating souls inside of them. It all seemed, to the members of the church, to add to the facade. And it didn't help that every time the ladies at the church would invite Jorja Sweet and her daughters to this kid's birthday party, or to attend this soiree, or that women's club meeting, she'd make up a likely excuse to explain why they could not attend.

Eventually, the church ladies began to think that Jorja Sweet thought she was too good for them and that she believed her three girls were too precious to cohort with the likes of their children, so the invitations stopped coming. Jorja Sweet never once told them that her husband just might snatch off the table leg of the dining room table and beat the crap out of her like he did the first and only time she had gone out and stayed too long. They had only been married for three months then, and she had never gone out with the girls again.

As critical as they were of her, not one of the ladies at the church who harbored unwarranted jealousy would have been able to fathom or endure the abuse Jorja Sweet suffered at home. She was not permitted to think for herself; Grey Samuel dictated her every move and defined her reason for existing. No one could have suspected that at home Jorja Sweet was not permitted to speak above a whisper. So if they wondered why her voice had all of a sudden become so mousy when as a child she was so rambunctious and outgoing, it was because she was afraid to speak any louder than he allowed her to, even outside of the house.

At home she kept her voice soft and as sweet as she could muster through her chronic nervous disposition because the wrath for breaking that rule was severe. Outside of the house, though less jittery because she was out of his reach, she still sustained the whisper for fear that if she raised its tone to a volume that people didn't have to strain to hear, they would somehow detect her secrets.

And those secrets buried themselves deep into the walls of 311 Highland Avenue and ate at the very structure of the house from the inside out like crazed, starving termites. And there were as many secrets as there were rules. And the slightest deviation from those rules was sure to be corrected with Grey's uncompromising hand. But there was no guarantee that doing everything exactly the way she was told would stop him from whipping her either. Still she had memorized every rule and repeated them mindlessly to herself so that she would never forget. As she gave birth to their children and as the girls grew old enough to understand, she made sure that they knew the rules too.

And the whispers continued. The girls were never allowed to run and jump and squeal like children do. The quiet in the house was deafening and as unnatural as the depraved acts that her husband would later perpetuate upon his own daughters. Jorja Sweet and her three daughters were not allowed to close themselves behind their bedroom doors in privacy either. In fact, they could not close themselves behind any door in his house, including the bathroom. She and her daughters were made to shower, shit and shave with no privacy at all. The closed doors from Grey's own childhood haunted him, so in his own house the rules had changed and the doors remained open throughout so that he could keep a close watch over his girls.

Some of the rules were strange, and somewhat cruel. Jorja Sweet and her girls couldn't use more than five panels of toilet paper to wipe away whatever wastes left their bodies. Dinner was expected to be on the table by 6:00 p.m. every single evening. And she cooked every day because she was not allowed to make enough for leftovers. Grey Samuel did not like twice warmed food, and that was just how it was. And when meals were served, she had to serve her husband first and allow him to complete his meal before she was permitted to call her girls to the table to eat. No one could eat before Grey Samuel had his fill, and he preferred to eat alone.

Jorja Sweet walked on eggshells in her house, trying desperately not to trouble the waters, but sometimes it only took Grey to have a bad day at work and she was sure to pay for it. And when he was drinking, he'd focus his abusive behavior on the girls. Besides the occasional whipping with his belt, his abuse of the girls did not manifest in the form of punches and bruises, and that was the secret Jorja Sweet protected the most. And it was the filthiest of her secrets because it involved Grey's improper conduct with his very own daughters.

Every single one of those women at Greater Good wanted the life they believed Jorja Sweet had. After all, she and her daughters seemed to be taken very good care of. They always looked polished and proper, shiny and new being driven around town by her fine husband in their fine clothes. They barely made eye contact with anyone, sat straight ahead, perfectly poised, back straight, hands folded in their laps and acting as demure as any Queen of England. Appearances can be deceitful because in truth they were as lifeless as any porcelain doll, that is, if anyone had bothered to see.

While Jorja and her daughters were regularly in sight, Grey's sightings were far fewer. They knew nothing about him because he was not from the neighborhood and did not belong to their church. That never stopped those gossiping women from speculating about who he must be, what he was like and about why he did not attend church with them. Without knowing him in the slightest and so offended by the change in Jorja Sweet, they sided with Grey by offering an excuse for his elusive behavior and assumed that since Jorja Sweet didn't even work – just sat at home being Joan Cleaver – he must have to work like a mule.

They all worked and contributed to their households, few Black women in their generation had the luxury not to. They assumed that on top of becoming snooty, Jorja Sweet must have also become a spoiled brat whose refusing to work forced her doting husband into long hours, six days a week, so Sundays were his only day to rest. How else could Jorja Sweet afford such nice things? They bet that he was simply obeying an insistent wife and forgave him of his indiscretions because even God had an off day. And in the same breath, they would condemn her for working the poor man to death.

Greater Good was a church settled from the sacrifices of twelve families, all of whom had migrated from Macon, GA and had established the church decades before. They also settled into the neighborhood around it, thus becoming staples in the community of Corryville too. Those twelve families, being the founding members of the church, were for several generation the only members of the church. And so, quite naturally, because their offspring were being raised together in the community of Greater Good, in such close living vicinity, coupling among them was inevitable. It was always the case that if there was a wedding being held at Greater Good, it was somebody's son and daughter from the congregation who would be the ones standing at the altar.

But Jorja Sweet had gone and married some man from somewhere else and he was all they could talk about. His mystery was infectious. They couldn't get enough of Grey Samuel. He had grown up in

Lincoln Heights and that was on the other side of town from Corryville, a distance too far to travel for any of them to have business there. Besides, those were uppity Black folk, self-professed suburbanites who had grown up in the inner-city neighborhoods but somehow had forgotten their roots when they moved into the middle-class and relocated to the first Black suburb. It was a self-believed fact that the residents of Lincoln Heights never let anyone forget.

Grey was an anomaly to them, which made him interesting, and by interesting that meant talked about. Musings about him consumed the conversations of the residents of Corryville, swirled like disturbed dust particles being swept off the ground. They talked about him in the barbershops and hair salons, while standing in line at the grocery store, and in around their dining tables during Sunday dinners with the family. Who he was and where he had come from was sure to be on the tips of tongues regularly.

They wondered how he got his good job at the hospital; they'd heard he was even some kind of manager. It might have been the same old shuck and jive Black people had always done – cleaning up after folks who are too lazy or too sick to clean up after themselves – but he had worked his way up to telling somebody under him how to mop a floor instead pushing the mop around himself. Manager meant in charge of something, and in Corryville, that was something to talk about. But most of all, they chattered about how he had changed Jorja Sweet into thinking her and her family were better than them, and the distaste with which the Samuel family was regarded grew with each spotting of them always sitting straight up and straight forward. They just couldn't imagine to what place the spirit of Jorja Sweet had flown away.

As a child and through her budding years, Jorja Sweet was what some might call engaging. She spoke with confidence about everything and anything she had an opinion about. She was her parent's pride and joy. She was smart and witty, as pretty as she was sweet, and could sing like a lark. To see her now walking around the church with her daughters whispering to each other and barely making eye contact with people directly in their paths of vision, was more than the church folks' Christian understanding could discern or tolerate.

The only thing that had remained in-tact about this hollow shell of a woman that barely resembled any inkling of the bubbly girl they had watched grow up was her voice. Jorja Sweet sang so loud and from the core of her belly every Sunday from the raised choir stand that she often went home with a raspy voice. Singing was the only thing that gave her any release from the quiet screaming in her head. Her Sunday singing replaced her constant crying, and helped her to endure each week ahead.

She just didn't belong to the neighborhood anymore.

The members of the church wondered why she had even bothered to stay there. Her newfangled attitude suggested that the better move would have been for her to go to Lincoln Heights, where this perfectly taupe complexioned man of hers had come from. But in lieu of any hint from Jorja Sweet, they could only presuppose that she must have refused to sell her parents' home because she had never left it even after they had died, and like a good husband, Grey must have been simply appeasing a demanding wife.

The home the Samuel family lived in had belonged to Jorja Sweet's parents and they had been a couple who, by all accounts, were said to have been made for one another. Jorja Sweet was 19-years-old when they left this earth exactly how they had lived – together. And the neighborhood and the church had tried to reach out to her. She had been broken, and it was the duty of good Christians to give her support. But they never had the chance to comfort her. For three months after the bodies of her parents were laid to rest Jorja Sweet stayed locked up in her house. Every curtain was drawn shut, every door secured with deadbolts, and at night not even a sliver of light shone throughout the entire two floor structure.

The only visitor she had allowed was Grey, who at the time was even more of a stranger to them. It was like he appeared out of the thin air one day on her doorstep and had never left. Her neighbors would watch him come and go, peaking out through partially opened curtains so as not to have their spying detected. He'd come bearing meals, flowers, bags of groceries and whatever else was needed to nurse Jorja Sweet back from her depression. And he would stay all night, coming out of the house in the dusk when the sky is pink with the first streaks of sunlight, getting into his car and remaining unseen again until the evening. When she finally emerged again from the house, Jorja Sweet looked well and he was given the credit for saving her.

But everything that looks good isn't always that pretty. None of the indignant and coveting women could have imagined that she was being beaten almost daily. Grey learned early on not to hit her in the face so the bruises never showed. But he didn't always leave bruises. Sometimes, he'd just put Jorja Sweet over his lap and whip her with one of his heavy leather belts, the same way he liked to whip the girls, except he'd make the girls undress down to their panties before laying across his lap for their lashing. When one did something wrong, they would all be punished for it. And no one ever asked and Jorja Sweet never said. The deductions, the lies, the whispers, and the secrets were never-ending. It was like having a real soap opera being played out before their eyes and was all the drama any of them could stand.

So many secrets swirled around in the smothering air between the walls of that house; violent secrets. But back then Black people didn't talk openly to other people about the business of their households. And that secrecy is the single protecting factor of the cycles of abuse that were allowed to continue and grow like an oxygen-exposed cancer throughout the Black community. Back then, Black women thought that only White women ran to a shrink, a marriage counselor, or to the police if their husbands were abusing them and their children, but it was a generationally accepted, well known fact that Black women had been taught to grin and bear it if he was a providing man.

The beautiful Billie Holiday said it best in her song "Nobody's Business" The lyrics spoke directly to Jorja Sweet's situation:

But I'd rather my man would hit me
Than allow him to jump up and quit me
Ain't nobody's business if I do
I swear I won't call no copper
If I'm beat up by my papa
Ain't nobody's business if I do
Nobody's business
Ain't nobody's business
Nobody's business if I do

Jorja Sweet blamed only herself; not her parents' sudden departure, not God, not the ladies of the church. She had been the one to marry a man she barely knew. She had been the naïve damsel in distress all too willing to believe the first man who ever pursued her was some kind of angel whose arrival was everything more than a stranger being kind. She, and only she, chose to surrender every ounce of her once undeniable confidence and allowed it to be replaced with fear. She feared every moment in his presence, every moment when she was alone, and while she hated almost every second of her days, she hated for him to come home the most.

Hearing his footsteps on the wood-floored foyer each evening gave Jorja Sweet the sickest feeling in her gut. She learned to predict what kind of night it was going to be by the sound of his walk. If he was in a foul mood, his feet would come down hard on the heel of his shoe and end with a sharp tap as the balls of his feet met the oak. This was an indication that Grey would be cursing and slinging insults and fists all night. If he was sullen, he'd drag each foot slow and deliberate across the floor as if he was trying to carve imprints in the wood. This was Jorja Sweet's way of knowing that he'd sulk and drink until he got an itching for a visit with one of her girls. Grey would do his sloppy business, stumble to the bed they shared smelling like whisky and the milk of pubescent sex and pass out next to her.

If she were any kind of woman, she'd slice his throat while he snored and slobbered, then grab her babies and run like hell until her life was too far in the distance for her to see. But she wasn't that kind of woman. She was a weak excuse for a mother, a battered wife to a drunken child molester; and albeit an unwilling participant, she still played victim to circumstances she never tried to stop. She was far from being any kind of woman. She reminded herself of that every day. So anything any of those ladies at Greater Good had to say about her was minuscule compared to the self-scolding she gave to herself.

Jorja Sweet had mastered the art of keeping things to herself. She held her secrets against her breasts like she wished she could hold her little girls; protectively and tight. She told nobody how he fondled them, or how he would come into their rooms some nights and make them take their little panties off right before their nightly baths so he could smell and lick on the crotch areas. She never, ever told anyone how he laid with them some nights, how he made them touch him with their little hands, how he made them watch him bathe while he fondled his penis, and how, just as they'd neared the age when boys start to take notice, he'd made them promise not to have sex with any boy before they had sex with him. He wanted to be the first one to show them how it should feel.

They promised because they were afraid not to and he threatened Jorja Sweet that if she ever told, he'd kill her. It was a timeless threat used by abusers to control the abused, but she believed he would do it if he decided he wanted to. So she gave her girls to him because she didn't think there was anything else she could do. She surrendered their innocence to him in hopes that he'd beat and rape her less often. She considered it rape because after he'd first started touching her girls, she never again desired him. He just took what he wanted anyway and as if it could be some consolation, Grey justified his behavior by promising that he would never ejaculate inside of them. But the promises of a pervert aren't worth shit.

Grey was a man obsessed with rules, and molesting his daughters was no different. He had a very specific method to his madness and he stuck to it with conviction, like most sociopaths. As each girl turned 5-years old, an age too young to understand what was happening to them but old enough to know that it wasn't right, she was granted a sneak preview of their father's perversion. He'd sit them on his lap and make them straddle his knee while he bounced them up and down. By the time they were 8, he was touching their private parts while he stroked his penis to erection and then finally to ejaculation. When they'd turned 10, he would put his fingers inside of their vaginas and kiss and suck the places where their breasts were supposed to be but had not begun to grow. And by the time they were 12 and as their figures began to react to the hormones of puberty, the fondling and touching progressed to penal penetration. His full grown penis was too big for their unopened vaginas that were barely covered with hair, but he'd taken their virginity anyway.

But somehow he had forgotten to hold back with Charlotta, and Jorja Sweet couldn't figure out why he'd done it. Maybe it had gotten good to him and over the years since he'd started molesting her, he'd fallen in love with Charlotta. After all, Charlotta had filled out beautifully with perfectly round breasts that were easy to hold, silver dollar nipples that seemed to remain erect and peak out from under all of her blouses, and an ass and hips that men were sure to fantasize about gripping. She had a slim, long neck, and a heart shaped mouth that was accentuated by the mole at its corner. Jorja Sweet had a mole in exactly the same place. She was beautiful. Maybe that's why he'd forgotten that she was his little girl and not his wife. Charlotta's small waistline completed the hourglass figure possessed but it would, however, soon be stretched to its capacity with child. The unthinkable happened, the other shoe dropped and landed with an incredible thud right in the middle of their madness.

When Jorja Sweet realized that the supply of maxi pads under the bathroom sink was not being depleted at the regular pace, she gathered all of her girls in the living room and sat them on the sofa. Charlotta was 15-years-old, Carmen was 13, and Camille was 11. She didn't whisper a word. She just looked at them deep in their eyes and scanned their faces for the slightest hint of that motherly glow that newly pregnant women seem to acquire. And when her eyes met Charlotta's, she knew. Her little girl Charlotta, the one who had suffered with her the longest, the oldest and the one who looked more like her than either of the other two, was with child. His child! She was carrying a child that would be her sister and her daughter, whose aunts would also be its sisters, and whose father would also be its grandfather.

Jorja Sweet didn't have to ask to know that Grey had done what he promised he'd never do. He'd released his seed inside of one of the girls, and that was the storm that crumbled the dam. Jorja Sweet's wail was so loud that the walls of the house, not used to absorbing anything close to its sound, seemed to shake. She questioned Charlotta with a fierceness she had not intended.

"What did he do?" she screamed and cried at the same time, shaking Charlotta by the shoulders until she shook her tears loose too.

Charlotta lied, "It's not his mama! I swear! It's a boy's at school."

Jorja Sweet wanted to believe that Charlotta's lie was true. But she knew; she just knew. Still, it would be just another secret to sweep under the rug, to hide behind the whispers. Jorja Sweet had screamed about it that one time only and then there was silence again. The screams retreated into her head and stayed there forevermore.

In retrospect, Jorja Sweet knew that the pregnancy

would change things. He had left Charlotta alone, cold turkey, the day she started showing. Maybe finally seeing the repulsive, callused proof of his sickness was too much for even someone as mean and as sick as Grey Samuel to handle. It was right around that time that he'd started drinking heavily and daily, which affected his ability to have an erection, so eventually he left the other girls alone too. He didn't desire Jorja Sweet anymore either and she was ecstatic about that. Jorja Sweet thought that her prayers had finally been answered.

Charlotta's pregnancy saved them all. There was no more abuse; not one more Samuel girl would have to suffer anymore. Even the unborn child was going to be spared of the sexual abuse at least. The seedling growing inside of her was Charlotta's child, but it also belonged to him. So, if Grey had been operating with all his cylinders when the unborn child passed through her stages of development, he would surely have had his way with her too. No doubt, she would have been introduced to the Daddy Grey way. Luckily for them though and thanks to his daily bottle of Wild Turkey, Grey had finally been castrated.

Jorja Sweet had allowed herself to believe that since he was now broken, she might actually, finally, have some peace and maybe even recover some of the happiness she faintly remembered before she married him. It was wishful thinking, maybe even delusional, but it filled her up with hope for her and for her family. In spite of the circumstance, Jorja protected her secrets even more fiercely than before. As long as no one knew the worst of the details and as long as they could only guess, it wasn't going to be real for Jorja Sweet either.

Through it all, conversations about the Samuel family continued as commonly in the homes of their neighbors as the delivery of their mail. And when Charlotta's belly began to push out from under her Sunday dresses, the conversations increased in fabrication and frequency. They knew that Charlotta's baby did not belong to any of their sons because they had been adamantly forbidden to court either of those Samuel girls. But Jorja Sweet wasn't saying, so there was no way to substantiate anything beyond that one fact. Still, what they could confirm just from looking was that Grey Samuel kept his women on a very short leash. No one had ever known him to allow anyone to get too close to his girls. So who the father of Charlotta's baby was became the most incessant of the conversations they'd ever had about the Samuels.

Corryville was the kind of neighborhood in which nothing happened without its residents knowing; who came in and who left out, which wives spent too much time with other women's husbands, whose furniture or car were being repossessed, and who had out of town guest confirmed by the unknown vehicles that were parked for more than a day in driveways. So, they knew that there had not been a boy from some other neighborhood frequenting the doorstep of the Samuel home. Jorja Sweet grew more obscure by the day, and her elusiveness made it hard not to make up stories about what they thought was going on. The conversations were only theories and indicative of the kind of gossip that gets juicier and juicier with every narrative shared among the storytellers over time.

And when Charlotta's baby came out looking more like Grey than Grey looked like himself, with no trace of genetics from any bloodline other than their own. When no boy ever materialized claiming fatherhood over the baby, the rumors didn't seem to need any further evidence to be able to hold water. It had been confirmed. Something weird was definitely going on.

And while everyone else grew increasingly more talkative, the whispers in the Samuel home grew in leaps over the chatter. They walked around each other whispering and keeping secrets. And even when Charlotta gave life to Grey's seed, despite Jorja Sweet's concentrated prayer that she would miscarry, there were still whispers and no one ever told. That seed, eventually birthed and named Merci, and where she had come from was the biggest secret of all. Merci was born, but had never lived as far as Jorja Sweet was concerned. She didn't hate the child, she just couldn't ever acknowledge who and what she was.

Her parentage was never discussed among the family. For the first 15 years of her life, Merci grew up knowing that something was wrong, but no one would tell her what the heaviness and the strangeness in her family was all about. Merci grew up aware of the dysfunction, but had been unexposed to its root, and it was maddening. She developed the same secret holding, whispering, indirect eye-contact and screaming in her head that had plagued her entire family, but their internal yelling was a direct result of the guilt and shame of knowing, Merci's was of confusion and pain.

With the natural instinct that only a child can possess because their third eyes has not yet been closed by the harsh realities of this world, Merci understood that her family was a mess. She, like her grandmother, her mother and her aunts (or sisters depending on which way a person was looking at it on a certain day) had grown up afraid of Grey Samuel, but they knew full well why he was to be feared and Merci hadn't a clue. She just always knew it, could always feel like she was supposed to be afraid of him too, even though by the time that she was nine-years-old, Grey Samuel was sick with sclerosis of the liver, a penis that did not work and a bad heart probably caused from all the hate stored in it over the years.

Like when the other Samuel girls were growing up, Merci was neither allowed to play and jump around when she had to stay in her grandparent's home after school. She hated being there waiting for Charlotta to get off work to come and save her. Sadly, it was not Grey who was making the demands, but Jorja Sweet who continued to enforce his rules, a side-effect suffered by many abused women. He was still ruling her though he wasn't even in any control of his own facilities. For the first years of Merci's life, he worked, came home and ate his dinner at the table alone, then retired to his room to drink a bottle of liquor and moan from the pain of his liver rotting from the inside out.

The only time Merci could remember seeing any real power in him was the time she was six-years-old. They had picked Merci up after school on her first day in first grade, and he had slapped Jorja Sweet while he steered his car along the route to their home. Merci had not known if it was her squealing report about her first day of school or something her grandmother had done that had set him off, but she'd quickly discerned that he was in charge.

Merci finally had proof that she should be afraid of her grandfather and it was no longer just a sense that he was the cause of whatever was wrong in her family. It was obvious in the way Jorja Sweet, and her mother and aunts walked around acting scared all the time and constantly reminding one another to do one thing or another the way they knew Daddy Grey expected. Even though he was pretty much incapacitated from the constant dialysis he was undergoing, he still yielded tremendous power over them from his sick bed.

He died when Merci was nine-years-old. He died in his bed all alone though everyone was home when he took his last breath. The rule he'd made that no one was to bother him once he retired to his room had been the reason no one knew he was lying in there having a heart attack. He was gone but nothing had changed. There still existed all around her adults who did not talk to her but who secretly talked all around her about her, barely looking at each other head on. And if that was not enough to destroy a child's self-esteem, the way she found out what all the whispering was all about was surely enough to destroy her spirit forever.

One Sunday morning, Charlotta rose slowly from her pew and reached for the microphone as the minister walked towards her on his way to the next person in line for a testimonial. Jorja Sweet instantly knew that the walls were getting ready to crumble around her. She sat in the choir stand eyeing her daughter curiously as Charlotta simply stated, "I had my father's baby. Can I or he be forgiven for that?" Grey Samuel had been dead for seven years by that time, but he was still running the show from the grave.

She then handed the microphone back to the minister and sat back down in her seat, as if she had not just caused major calamity and shock, as if she could not hear the gasps and frightful "Oh my

God's" rising and falling inside the church's sanctuary. Several minutes had passed before an absolutely inaudible hush strangled the congregation. No one moved a muscle and Jorja Sweet sat glued to her seat waiting to see what everyone else would do.

When no one did anything, the minister gathered his composure, cleared his throat and moved on to the next parishioner. Jorja Sweet simply got up, left the choir stand, and grabbed Charlotta by the hand as she passed her pew on the way out. She motioned to Carmen and Camille, who sat just a few pews behind to get up and follow. By the time that the Samuel parade was passing Merci, who sat on the pew at the back of the church reserved for the senior and junior ushers and the church nurses, she knew to bring up the rear of the procession without needing to be told. The strange quiet that had descended onto everyone reshaped the remainder of the service. It never quite made it back to the normal volume of praise that morning like Greater Good was accustomed to.

Though Jorja Sweet yelled a million times in her mind over the years at the knowing, she had always maintained poised in public. She was so used to putting on a charade, it felt as if she'd never done anything other than that. The yelling in her head was ceaseless but it never made it from her thoughts to her words. Jorja Sweet stayed in character for more than a decade and a half after Merci took her first breath. And she would have been able to keep the performance up, had she not been betrayed by her eldest child, who by the time she told the world, was a grown ass woman and should have known better.

Betraying the family code of "don't tell even if asked" was unthinkable and for as long as Jorja Sweet was concerned for the rest of her years, it was unforgiveable. She had worked too hard, had suffered too long, had sacrificed too much for it all to come to an unfixable end. Jorja Sweet prayed every remaining living day that Charlotta would have nothing but grief in her life, and that her eldest, most knowing daughter would have to suffer and sacrifice ten times more than she ever did. Until the day the Samuel girls put their mother in her grave, Jorja Sweet could daily be heard whispering into the thin air in her home that Charlotta was a traitor.

The whispers had finally been heard, the secrets had finally come oozing out of the cracks in the walls of the family's well-protected fortress. Still Jorja Sweet refused to believe, to accept, or to utter a word to anyone but herself. Jorja Sweet had grown old overnight, worn, tired, and weak; not sick just beat down by life. She hoped her days were numbered. At this point, what could she do? From the moment the secret was revealed, she walked out of Greater Good, back straight and head held high just as they had come to know her to be, and never stepped foot across its threshold again. The only one in the family who ever went back was Carmen, and she carried on the charade for them all.

And when it had all come rushing out like a waterfall slamming into a shaky dam and breaking through the barrier as easily as if it were made of loose sand, Merci felt like the joke was on her because she was just finding out with the rest of Greater Good what everybody she'd called family had always known all her life. She could not believe that her kinfolk, though strange and somewhat distant, could have let her find out that way. Her life felt like one big, fat, ugly, rotten lie!

And those same gossipy, self-righteous neighbors stopped being disappointed in Jorja Sweet to pity her; the disdain, however, continued. She was on one hand sadly locked up in her parent's house impelled to the prison her husband had planned for her, and on the other, a repulsive woman and terrible mother for allowing her husband to abuse their daughters. And now with clear evidence, their stories would never be perceived as rumors again. And now that they knew, they felt entitled to be disgusted. Sixteen years of assuming had been made to feel completely worth it when, at last, they could point the finger and be justified in doing so.

And though their knowing should have explained Jorja Sweet's isolation, her excessive involvement in the church, and the overall change she seemed to have undergone since she was the little girl they all remembered but also had forgotten, they never invited her back into the protective fold of the community. They were not happy about the perversion that had slithered its way into their neighborhood thanks to the shameful and sinful behavior going on in her home; not Grey's home, but Jorja Sweet's home. They were not happy to have been forced to explain such torrid, twisted behavior to their own children whose questions became constant in the light of the discovery. Jorja Sweet and all her girls – all four, Charlotta, Carmen, Camille and yes, even Merci – would forever be outsiders, then and now by no choice of their own.

It's funny how one family's secrets can shred the very fabric of a whole community of people into pieces of frazzled thread, especially when the secrets were the kind of enormous iniquity that could not be ignored. Turning a blind eye to them only added a lie to the lie, and strings of lies only produced a worthless ball of bullshit.

CHAPTER 4: COMING HOME

It has always been said that home is where the heart is, but for some that sentiment couldn't be farthest from the truth. Merci had left her heart, along with the rest of who she used to be, in Cincinnati almost a decade and a half ago and she'd never planned to return. She was only now reluctantly taking the journey back, at the age of 35, because her mother had died. Charlotta Samuel was being laid to rest and if her only child did not see fit to attend her funeral, people would surely think that her soul was truly damned. It was not any religious conviction of her own that drove Merci to concede, Merci had never had much of a reason to believe. She was there only because she knew it was the right thing to do, or at least, it was surely what she'd thought the long forgotten people of her long ago life would expect.

Driving south on I-71, approaching Kings Island Amusement Park, it did not even remotely feel like a place that she'd ever want to admit was once the place she called home. Merci stared blankly at the bright blue sign flashing the name Paramount above the words Kings Island and realized that the infamous senior skip day location had undergone some changes; or at least a name change. She wondered what else had changed. Maybe nothing would be the same as it had been when she'd hot-tailed it out of there all those years before, and that gave Merci a faint hope, although short lived, that maybe this first return trip back to the place she was born wouldn't hold with it the pain she'd left behind.

Seeing the attraction where she'd spent her own senior skip-day with her graduating class from Withrow High School did not, however, evoke good memories. Merci had spent that entire day riding the roller coasters alone because, by then, everybody knew her truth. It sadly reminded her that the more things change, the more they stayed the same. She was alone then, and it was silly of her to think that something as stupid as the name change of some amusement park made her any less alone now.

A few minutes later, she steered the car passed the Montgomery Road exit. The scenery was slowly becoming a little more familiar, and that nauseated her. Merci resisted the urge to regurgitate and paint the dashboard with the chicken breast sandwich and grape soda she had packed for the 11 hour drive from New York, but had just eaten coming through Columbus, OH. Her tightly knotted stomach twisted in disapproval and all but chastised her for being here.

Merci rubbed her belly to calm it, but to no avail. She wished, for a brief moment, that she had decided to fly instead of drive. At least on a plane she could go to the bathroom, stick her finger down her throat, and relieve the swimming feeling now making her want to gag. She would have flown, but couldn't endure one more delayed or cancelled flight, one more lost piece of luggage or over-booked and over-crowded plane. Nor did she feel like dealing with the airline representatives who had less than friendly attitudes and always seemed to sling responses to passengers' questions with more condescension than any customer service professional should.

The last time she had flown over three years before, Merci had found herself stuck in DC's Washington Dulles International Airport for twelve hours, into the ridiculously wee hours of the morning waiting on a flight crew to arrive whom Merci swore never existed until the airline found a few insomniac pilots and flight attendants to manage the flight. The forgotten group of passengers that sluggishly boarded the plane at 2:00 a.m. had been just too exhausted to worry about where this crew had come from and whether or not it was safe to be 35,000 miles above the surface of the earth with them at that hour. Thinking of it now, Merci got pissed all over again.

Aside from the dozens of delayed and cancelled flights that inconvenience passengers daily, Merci hated most of all the overly sensitive security measures being taken to combat America's fear of terrorism. In her opinion, the Middle Eastern zealots who used their religion to justify hate, did not seem stupid enough to use a plane for their future acts of terror. And besides, if America would just stay out of those people's dealings, they'd all be safer. To Merci, this business with the taking off of shoes and not being able to take more than 3 ounces of liquid onto a plane seemed more of a punishment to the Americans it was trying to protect than to the foreigners they were trying to keep out. So Merci opted to save herself the headache. She borrowed her friend, Karissa's Ford Focus to save on the gasoline expense, and left her oversized, over-compensating Hum-V in New York. At least this way she could be alone with her thoughts for a while to try to prepare for what lie ahead.

Besides, Karissa's two year old vehicle barely had 5,000 miles on it. She was a New York native and therefore had a preference for the city's elaborate and perfectly sufficient transportation system. Karissa had only accumulated that many miles on her car from the monthly trips she took to Philadelphia to see her mother. But Merci's 3-year-old SUV, on the other hand, had almost 50,000 miles on it. She drove everywhere almost all the time, and when Merci wasn't driving she was in a cab. These were expenses she budgeted for and for which she sacrificed in place of things like the weekly pedicures and manicures that Karissa and every other professional woman she had met in New York City indulged themselves with. Hell, the home-mani/pedi kit she had bought worked just fine and no one was the wiser.

For Karissa and every other die-hard New Yorker, going to and from work, running daily errands and traveling for any need that included some distance, taking the train or a bus was first nature and first choice. Driving and risking the chance of having to circle the city blocks for what seemed like hours looking for a place to park, or paying a ridiculous amount of money to park in a garage was something that simply did not make sense to most of the people Merci knew throughout all five boroughs, but she could care less how much of transplant driving her car everywhere made her look. Merci was determined to put good use to the vehicle she paid $550 a month to have.

Karissa Sherman was the first friend that Merci made when she arrived in New York City, thirteen years before. They were both 22 years old and fresh out of college. Karissa and Merci had met in the hair salon both getting expensive styles of braids that neither of them could afford on their newly employed budgets, but had decided to splurge on themselves anyway. Right away the common thread in their personalities had been found and tied together, and they began hanging tight like they had been childhood friends. It was 1993 and the world had already experienced and survived the first attack on the World Trade Center. And now in 2006 and several years after the second attack that would come to be known simply as 9/11, their friendship was still standing unlike the twin towers.

When Merci first announced that she would not be coming home after her college graduation and that she was opting instead to move to the big city, her family had not understood why she wanted to live in New York in the first place, and after the second time in recent history of it having been the target of terrorism, it became less apparent to Merci's Aunt Carmen why she chose to stay. As far as it concerned Carmen, New York City was a crazy cesspool of sin and vile living, and the cost of living was ridiculous, literally and figuratively.

But Merci had set her sights on the city years ago. New York City was where she'd decided she wanted to be in her sophomore year of college after she'd visited for the first time. She and some of her college girlfriends, bored with the usual New Year's Eve celebrations in their respective towns, had decided not go home for the Christmas vacation and decided instead to catch a Greyhound to New York City to see the ball drop in Time Square. In those following two years that it had taken Merci to finish her degree, she would visit at least twenty more times and would eventually fall in love with the eclectic world of art and music and culture she experienced there.

And uptown Manhattan, better known as Harlem, was the borough in which she knew she'd live. Merci could envision herself stomping down the renowned 125th Street in and out of boutiques with one of kind styles hanging in the windows, or shaking her tail-feather in one the nightclubs on Lenox Avenue, or snapping at some basement open mic on Frederick Douglas Boulevard spitting heavy lyrics to a crowd of wine sipping, cigarette smoking artsy types. She saw herself among the bangle wearing, multi ring-bearing sisters who progressively sported locs and naturals of all sizes, and who adorned their bodies in the home-made clothes designed by the bohemian-like sister who owned the spot and fancied herself a seamstress of fashions that suited the artist/activists sisters they were. She dreamed about bedding one of the lyrically inclined men who wrapped their crowns in cloths big enough to be towels and tied in huge knots at the nape of their necks. Poetry spots were the only places where men could get away with wrapping their heads, and thanks to Russell Simmons it was cool again for brothers to recite poetry.

And Merci knew that as a lover of art and expression, and as an aspiring poet and writer who occasionally found the courage to read some of her poetry in front of a crowd, her spirit would be inspired in no better place. All the different colors of cultures and different colors of people blended and integrated against a concrete background that, despite the glass and brick, shined in a way that made the world recognize. New York City had a fire, a vibe that would never be denied, and Merci was itching to be a part of it.

New York City had everything she wanted. It was moving and shaking and dancing and creating and living without boundaries. It had water surrounding the shores of its five boroughs, which gave her an option, as the true Piscean woman that she was, to get close to the element to which she was mostly inclined whenever she'd want to. And if she traveled far enough North she could encounter the freshness of countryside so open and airy that she would swear she was in Indiana somewhere. She could have quick weekend get-a-ways from the city whenever her mind needed the rest. Merci was sure that she'd be able find a quaint little bed and breakfast up state to retreat to and write from time to time.

New York was also a cornucopia of available, straight black men who were as diverse as they were roughneck, as much conscious as they were hustlers, with a swagger that can only be attributed to that New York state of mind that Nas rapped about on his Illmatic CD. Unlike the thousands of gay Black men that populate and sashay through the streets of Atlanta like every day is Gay Pride, the men in New York just seemed to own their manhood and though she had no plans of ever marrying a single one of them, she knew she'd be able to get her world rocked whenever she'd want to. And in spite of her past, and because of her past, sex came easy. But love was another matter altogether; a matter Merci seldom allowed question or conversation about.

When she'd first determined that the east coast would be her residence, Merci made herself believe that it was all about her artistry and making a name for herself in the city of limitless possibilities. She was so young then and driven by the misty eyed hope of silly youth, green from having grown up in the reserved Midwest, and from being an only 22-year-old, barely out of college woman who'd never even had a job other than the one she had in the writing lab on her Midwest college campus. But eventually she had to make herself accept the truth; that the move to New York City was more about the fear of returning to her past than it was about finding her artistic greatness. She believed that if she put enough miles between her now and her before, it would finally just fade away. New York was just the kind of city to be in if you wanted to get lost, to lose something, or to lose someone. Merci's irrepressible desire to be as far away from everything she had ever known was more akin to her legacy than she knew.

Once after reading a short story she had written in college, her creative writing professor said that she'd be a remarkable writer when she finally and truly allowed herself the experience of speaking through the pain she kept hidden in her depths. But as far as it concerned Merci, her writing was not a tool she planned to waste on mending the holes in her life. Writing and performing were her escape away from her life; a life that could not be fixed anyway. Through the written median she intended to invite all kinds of characters to take up residence in her mind from where she could make them real to people. She could forever elude the world of her own narrative. She could create pictures of families she'd never known but always imagined must exist, images of men she never believed she'd know, and portraits of women who found entitlement in their womanhood instead of the women she knew who were mostly just victims of men. She secretly hoped that she could give life to so many amazing characters that her own pathetic existence could be overshadowed and eventually, permanently disappear.

Soon after getting to New York, however, she realized that hustling was as necessary to survival as breathing is to living. Merci had always dreamed of being a writer, but New York turned out not to be inspiration she'd hoped for. She was an itty bitty guppy in a huge, never ending ocean. Hers became a dream deferred. She didn't have time to chase dreams if she'd planned to have stability. Her first job was the only job she'd ever end up having. She'd been progressively successful at the same job for thirteen years, working her way to an earning that allowed her to live rather comfortably.

But in those first few years, the entry level salary she had begun her employment earning was too meager for her to go fluttering around New York trying to be a writer. Merci discovered that she'd much rather preferred to eat and have a warm apartment. She was not equipped to be a struggling artist and she was okay with that, so she emerged herself in a 9 to 5 at an established publishing company and toiled through her daily duties like most everyone else in the Big Apple. She enjoyed her job and had experienced quite a bit of success at Southall and

Weinstein Publishing, first as a copy editor and now as the senior editor for the newly acquired manuscripts of African American clientele whose books were now being written and shopped in waves of urban grit and romanticized stories of Black life.

Merci never got around to writing a story of her own. She settled instead to take a job helping other author's dreams come true. She seldom traveled the few blocks from her house to the clubs on Lenox, and hardly ever did much shopping in her own neighborhood, opting instead to shop in Manhattan and near her job in Columbus Circle. Besides, there were few boutiques left by the time Merci relocated there. The Harlem that Merci had fallen in love with in 1989 when she'd first visited had changed by the time she got there in 1993. The crack cocaine era had done a lot of damage to the areas that were heavily populated with a once thriving Black culture. The danger and crime that naturally came with the epidemic had ravished the neighborhoods quickly, but the war on drugs was just starting to take the streets back when she moved into her first cramped apartment. And though by the turn of the century things were mostly cleaned up, Harlem had lost its Black culture, changed by the arrival of President Bill Clinton and gentrification.

Occasionally however, despite how much Merci had to work to afford a comfortable lifestyle, she did have the chance to journey east on the Roosevelt and across the Brooklyn Bridge in search of the latest poetry spot in Brooklyn. Or sometimes she'd venture out to hear some live music at a local spot in Harlem when it was warm and she could enjoy a late night walk to get there. It was these venues where Merci could recite a self-composed poem or two, groove to the latest up and coming neo soul singer/songwriters trying to make it the big city, and feed her love for the arts just to keep her creativity from dying completely.

As if things could be any more different than she'd imagined, after having only been in the city for 2 years, she was attacked in the subway, which is the exact time she decided never to ride the subway again and began permanently relying on her own vehicle to get her to and fro. She stopped thinking that New York City was some kind of magic kingdom with the ability to tantalize all of her musings, and adjusted to the reality of the brick city she was in.

Merci's subway attacker was an ex-boyfriend who'd tackled her on a platform under the Port Authority, and tried to have sex with her right there in the middle of the day on a Saturday when the subway in Manhattan is bulging and threatening to pop at its seams. From that day forward, she vowed her subway days were over. She never rode the subway again. Leaving behind anything that hurt her had always come easy to Merci.

The attack was foreshadowed in the weeks that

proceeded. Her crazy ex, who just could not let it go, had been following her, calling her home at all hours of the night and early morning babbling about how their break up was killing him, and popping into her office at lunchtime to take her out for a bite pretending to everyone in the office that they were still an item.

Merci tried to pacify him and console his aching heart by explaining as gently as she could that she liked him, but she just didn't love him. She never explained that she didn't know how to love. Once his love started showing, she simply pushed him away. She had had more than her fair share of lovers who could not move on, so nothing about his behavior alarmed her. She just felt sorry for him like she did most of the men who were lured too deep into her abyss as if carried off downstream by a riptide. Most of the men in her past had been drawn in by her overwhelming beauty and crushed as if by hurricane size waves when they realized that she was unlovable.

Sure, the unexpected attack was an isolated incident, still it made her think about all the dangers that lurked in that sewer New Yorkers have the nerve to call public transportation, and she just could not do it anymore. Merci was the kind of woman who had a low tolerance for pain, especially the internally inflicted kind that was caused by men. Any place, situation, or circumstance that presented a threat of stripping her of control, were the kinds of places, circumstances and situations that she avoided at all costs. And any person, especially any man who tried to put her in a position to be victimized, were regarded by Merci as monsters who could slyly disguise themselves as human beings.

To make matters worse, the bastard who had tackled her on the subway had broken the heel of her brand new Michael Kors shoes, a purchase for which she had to sacrifice a whole lot of lunch money and tickets to the most attended old school jam in NYC held at the Roseland Ball Room that year. She had even had to pass on a concert at BB King's featuring her favorite singer, Erykah Badu.

The subway incident had scarred Merci emotionally, as always and this time, physically as well. She had skinned her arm so badly it took a month for the skin to regenerate itself and close the open wound, and left a scar that she had had to rub four times a day with cocoa butter to smooth out. The scar eventually shrunk and virtually disappeared under the softening magic of the butter. It took about three months before she could wear any shirt without full or three quarter length sleeves again, but she persisted with the daily application of the salve because she knew that the cocoa butter would not let her down.

So many so called African American geared cosmetic companies these days claim to have healing agents in their products, but Merci had never seen any that could do justice to the human skin like cocoa butter. Despite the many bumps and bruises that she had acquired from the occasional collision with a bed frame or the corner of a table, she was practically spotless. She contributed that to the daily use of cocoa butter, applied literally and liberally from head to toe. She'd starting using cocoa butter when she was in college because she liked the way it smelled. She later discovered how soft and smooth it made the skin and how it helped to heal little scars she'd get from shaving her legs. Hell, it worked so well, she wished somebody would come up with a cocoa butter for the soul; a salve to get rid of the callused parts, not just cover and soften the blemishes.

As she thought about the attack at that moment while steadily making her way down I-71, Merci folded her right arm across her chest and touched the spot on her left arm with the tip of her fingers. She lightly rubbed at the spot where the scar had been. It was just a faint line now that all but disappeared in the summer under the affects of the sun's kiss on her skin. It lay just above her elbow and extended along the backside of her arm almost to the crease where her arm folded to meet the armpit. She absent mindedly touched the spot and recalled how the actual humiliation of her skirt being pushed up to her waist and her panties being yanked to the side, exposing her closely shaved cha-cha to the two dozen New Yorkers who stopped to gawk but not to help, bothered her least of all. She was used to her outside being observed. As long as people couldn't see beyond her physical, her fragile parts could remain safe inside of her cocooned outer shell.

Merci had first been introduced to the uninhibited physical exposure as a small child. Whenever she visited her grandparent's home, she had been made to leave all doors in the house wide open at all times, even when she was showering in the bathroom or dressing in the guest room. And in the apartment that she and her mother lived in until the day Charlotta Samuel up and left, her mother walked around barely covered every single day. It was just her nature to be uninhibited.

Grey Samuel always had a thing about closed doors. Merci realized that now she did too. He hated them to be closed, and she hated them to be open. Everything about where she had come from had been internalized and then distorted into some numb state of existence for her. Every room with a door in her house stayed shut. The glow of natural sunlight from the huge picture windows in her third floor, studio style brownstone was never allowed to fill the openly structured apartment, and was kept at bay by beige colored, linen covered vertical blinds. Even at work, if she was in her office, the door was closed and the shades were drawn. She lived behind closed doors, both literally and figuratively, both physically and emotionally, and forever shutting out anyone who stood on the other side trying to get in.

Merci was finally pulling off the highway and creeping along a road she had erased from her memory long ago. But it seemed like she could eerily recall every iota of its curves and dips as she made her way along William Howard Taft Road, towards Highland Avenue and back to everything she'd spent the adult years of her life running from. A very tired Merci slowed the car at the corner as she prepared to make the right turn onto her old block and into the gates of hell. She'd swear if anyone asked that she'd heard the rattle of the metal bars slamming shut as soon as the vehicle had cleared the curb.

She had seen in her peripheral vision but did not really take notice of the mural that lined the south wall near the parking lot of what used to be Merry Junior High School. A flash of a distant moment streaked through her mind as if it was from a movie she had once seen as opposed to one that she had actually lived. It was in those halls that she had been fondled and first kissed open mouthed and with the use of tongues. The kiss had disgusted her at the time, and the smell of the boy's saliva on her upper lip made her want to throw up on him. But even though she had been slightly repulsed, puberty inevitably had control over her senses and bodily functions. The pulsating between her legs and moisture on her cotton panties embarrassed and confused her. How could she like it and hate it at the same time?

She wondered what the building was now since she

knew that most middle schools in Cincinnati ceased to exist by the time she graduated high school. The building had been vacated and locked up when she left here for college, but she figured that the revival of the mural had to mean the building was again being occupied. As she drove along the west side of her old school building, she saw that the sign on its nicely manicured lawn read Cincinnati Board of Education. Wow! She suddenly remembered the oddly colored, rust like building that used to house the Board of Education in downtown Cincinnati, just around the block from the Justice Center; or Just Us Center if you were asking one of the hard-knock young men who strolled the streets of Over the Rhine.

Diagonally across from the middle school used to be the corner store. Merci could not recall what the name of the store was or if she ever knew what it was, but she did, briefly, evoke the memory of stopping there almost every day on the way home from school to get barbecue Grippos potato chips, and a Welch's grape soda. Grape soda and barbecue chips were a staple in her life, so much so that she'd actually considered changing her mind about moving to New York City. She'd gotten over it when she found a comparable brand and so the obsession continued.

Even though the memories she had allowed herself seemed pleasant enough, Merci still did not want to be here. However, like most of her childhood choices, she was being directed by the needs of someone else. The mother that she had spoken to only off and on for the last 10 years had died. And if for no other reason than obligation, she was here.

Worse yet, she was expected to say something at the funeral. Hell, she was the daughter, the only daughter and the only offspring of her mother's siblings. Wasn't she the one who was supposed to sit on the front row instead of giving the eulogy? She would much rather be allowed to shrink on one of the pews and be falsely appreciative of the embraces being offered by fellow mourners. Although she must admit, she was grieving but not for the lifeless body of her mother's and not because she felt like she was losing anything. In fact, she felt like her life could finally begin now that her mother's soul had departed its earthly frame in search of its eternity. Merci's pain stemmed from the emotional abuse she was being forced to revisit and the disconnect she felt from the one person in the world who should have loved her better.

Merci wondered what her mother's eternity would be. Merci recalled from a religion class that she'd taken as an elective in college that the Quran says that sins will be punishable by degree. Did that mean Charlotta would suffer in everlasting loneliness and fear like she had caused her only child to do? Would Charlotta's eternity be the hell she had made Merci's life become? It's not that Charlotta Samuel was mean to her only daughter, she was just indifferent.

Merci could not understand why her mother behaved so strangely towards her. Charlotta was so sweet and kind to other people. She could be affectionate and was generally the life of the party when other people were around. But as soon as the living room door of their tiny ghetto apartment would close, putting company on the opposite side of it, Charlotta would retreat into a quiet, melancholy place into which she never invited Merci to follow.

And then when Merci turned 16 years of age, her mother's silence was finally broken. She would never understand how her mother had decided that the third row of the pews at Greater Good was a good place to finally break free of the silence. From the back pew she'd occupied she uncomfortably looked upon the scene and thought, "I wanted her to talk to me, but not like that!"

It still stunned Merci to think about the whole ridiculously awkward scene, one that no matter how far she ran, she would never forget the bomb her mother had dropped that fateful somber Sunday. And then six days later, she was gone. Charlotta had left her for where the family would later find out was a small parish in the southwestern region of Jamaica's shores, where she stayed for several years. Merci lived with her Aunt Carmen until she left for college one year after her mother left, and she hadn't had any need or reason to return to Cincinnati until now.

The car instinctively seemed to stop on its own as soon as it was parallel to her grandparent's home. The land on which the house was set seemed to sag, as if the house's foundation was too heavy, laden with the sum of all the sadness its walls held. Merci's own grief was really beginning to loom overhead now as if a dark and stormy cloud was suspended there, she almost expected to hear thunder clap loudly in her ears. The regular night sounds of crickets and the occasional night wind was nearly inaudible to Merci, and the near silence made her shrink in fear. Panic erupted at the thought of opening the car door and putting her feet on the sagging pavement. The weight of her sadness would surely make the ground under her give way. So she just sat there and tried to let the hum of the running car calm her.

Instead of calm, her mind, usually more merciful when she most needed it to be, wandered to the eulogy she had been elected to deliver. She had not come up with one word of it yet. Merci could not comprehend what she was supposed to say about Charlotta; this self destructive, yet undeservingly persecuted woman. Nor could she understand why she was being forced to speak those ever special words that would paint the memories of the funeral attendees rose-colored and send her mother's spirit into eternity in peace; those words that were supposed to grant Charlotta's restless soul some rest and forgiveness.

Maybe she had become the chosen one by default. Over the years, Merci was the only one who had tried to have some contact with Charlotta Samuel. Her sisters, Merci's aunts, Camille and Carmen, stopped calling when Charlotta decided to move back to Cincinnati and take up residence in their parent's house, despite the turmoil that was sure to come by re-opening those doors and letting its demons out.

Merci knew that she was getting ready to step back through the doors where those demons laid in wait, deep in the shadowy corners of every part of that house, excited to devour new flesh. She hoped that she had an armor substantial enough to keep them from getting through and eating her alive. She sat in the running car and initiated a prayer for the very first time in her life though she wasn't quite sure of how to refer to the entity she called herself praying to. Her prayer was quick and to the point. She asked for strength to get her through these next few days unscathed and for a rightful punishment to be handed down upon the soul of the woman who was still making her life hell.

CHAPTER 5: HELLO YESTERDAY

Merci stood on the wooden porch staring at the brass knocker in the center of the door, as if contemplating whether or not to reach out and bang it against the painstakingly maintained structure. Even if she had, no one would have answered because no one lived there but ghosts. Besides, she had the key and could have entered without knocking. She'd always had a key to her grandparents' house. She never gave it back when she left Cincinnati for college. She'd kept it for reasons she couldn't explain especially since she'd never planned to come back. She'd had to take almost everything out of the junk drawer in the kitchen of her brownstone to find it, but Merci knew it was there buried like everything else from her past.

Merci glanced at her watch and thought to herself that she'd made pretty good time. Taking note of the time, 9:12 p.m., she was puzzled. She couldn't recall, but silently questioned if she had driven above the speed limit the entire way. And if so, why had she been in a rush? She had left New York close around 11:30 that morning, shaving over an hour off of what was supposed to be an 11-hour drive. And now that she was there, staring at a closed door with a growing fear that was oddly familiar, she began to feel like it was a mistake to come. Nothing had changed; this house could still strike nauseating trepidation in her soul.

"Well, welcome home Merci." The thought had been aimlessly said aloud as if someone was standing next to her and had inquired. Merci's lips had moved without any will on her part, and the sound of her own voice gave her chill bumps all over her skin.

So present was the feeling that some other energy was controlling her present situation, Merci looked over her shoulder and half-way expected someone or something to be standing there. Satisfied that there were no spirits standing in the shadows, Merci refocused her attention back to the heavy wooden barrier standing between her present and past. Her anxiety increased ten-fold as she further contemplated putting the now sweaty key that she held tightly in her fisted hand into the lock and stepping into yesterday. It was all too much, causing her breathing pattern to increase and exasperating the swirl of emotions spinning in rapid succession inside her. She'd checked so her eyes knew that she was standing there alone, but Merci's mind swore it could feel a pushing at her back, strong like the wind in Chicago rolling inland off Lake Michigan in January.

Erykah Badu interrupted her progressively growing frantic state and startled Merci more than the feeling of the strange aura that had her heart in its grip. Realizing that the singing was coming from her purse, she reached inside and pulled out the ringing cell phone and felt grateful for the message the song was giving her...*on and on and on and on, my cipher keeps moving like a rolling stone*...she chided herself for forgetting that she had moved on from her past, it couldn't stop her now any more than it ever did.

She flipped the phone open. "Hello, this is Merci".

"Girl, if I were there with you, I'd kick your ass." Karissa was screaming through the receiver so loudly that Merci had to pull the phone a few inches away from her ear.

"What is wrong with you girl and where are you calling me from? This is not a number that my caller ID recognizes as one of yours." Merci waited for her friend to respond.

"No, mine are the only questions being answered right now. One, have you made it to Cincinnati, and two, why didn't you call me to check in during the ride?"

Karissa was acting like her protector, a role she had become accustomed to and fell into effortlessly. Merci had never told Karissa about her incestuous family and how damaged she was on the inside, but somehow this amazingly intuitive woman always sensed that Merci needed to be kept close in her sight and within her embrace.

"Calm down girl, I'm here. Why are you tripping?"

Merci wrapped her wisp-like voice in a little giggle to divert her friend from having a complete spasm. "I just really needed to take the ride in solitude, get my head straight. You know?"

Karissa smacked her lips and sighed her concession, "I get that girl, but a quick call from a gas station while you stopped to fill up somewhere halfway through Pennsylvania was all I would have needed to make those images retreat of you lying somewhere in some ditch after drifting off to sleep behind the wheel from the bored exhaustion of that ridiculously long and stupid drive. It was crazy for you to drive when you can afford to fly." Karissa often spoke in long, run on sentences, not stopping for a period until her whole point was understood.

"I'm sorry sis, I should have called." Merci was still standing on the porch of her great grandparent's house, still facing the door as if her feet had gotten stuck there. The silence that followed her apology relayed to Karissa that something was wrong.

"You okay?" Karissa's voice had softened to a soothing, motherly tone that gave Merci just enough courage to pull her feet from the planted position they had been in. She managed to turn around and sit on the top step of the porch before the tears started to swell in her eyes.

"Karissa, I don't think I can go in there. I'm not ready. Thirteen years and over nine hours of driving and I am still not ready." Merci wanted to cry, and though crying didn't come easy for her, she felt like she needed to relieve some of the pressure and a good cry was the only remedy that would work. Her insides were jittery, but Merci maintained the stillness in her voice. She didn't want to alarm her friend any further, so she sucked in her breath to steady the strain building in her throat and pull in the possible flow of tears. She had long ago learned how to manage her emotion and keep the composure of what some had to believe was the mark of her being a strong woman. But Merci's poise had little to do with strength and more to do with her relentless need to be in control.

"Don't do it then, girl." Karissa's response sounded so simple and sure in its resolve that Merci was instantly persuaded. "Didn't you say you had to view the body at the funeral home tomorrow?"

"Yeah, I believe my Aunt Carmen said the appointment is at 9:00 a.m." Merci's near breakdown was subsiding quickly with every word that Karissa offered.

"Well, if nothing is happening this evening that needs your attention, there doesn't seem to be any reason to jump in right now. Check into a hotel for the night, if you think you'll be more comfortable. You had a long drive. The least you can do tonight is to have a drink and a restful sleep before things get crazy."

As usual, Karissa had the answer Merci wanted to hear. "You're so right. I'd feel safer in a hotel. This house is too big for me to sleep in alone."

She knew she'd covered up the real reason why she couldn't manage to get the key in the lock, but Merci needed to hold off the inevitable for just a little while longer. She pealed her butt off the porch and almost ran the length of the walkway back to the car. If the neighborhood hadn't changed as much as it seemed to have, The Vernon Manor Hotel would be just around the corner, and though it was less than an eighth of a mile from where she was, Merci couldn't get there fast enough. She and Karissa said their goodnights and made promises to be in touch before the weekend ended, and Merci pulled away from the Samuel house finally relieved.

Merci drove the short distance between Highland Avenue and Oak Street to the Vernon Manor Hotel and was checked in and soaking in a bubble bath by 10:30 p.m. The Manor Inn was a small privately owned hotel that resembled the quaint feeling of a bed and breakfast. Though it was not a franchised chain like Greaters ice cream and Larossa's pizza, it had been a staple in the community since she was a little girl. Despite being in the middle of its urban surrounding, the Vernon Manner maintained the dignity of exclusivity. It still had the same neat and antique-decorated rooms as it always had.

The tub that Merci lay stretched out in was an old school, porcelain tub with legs that elevated it about two inches off the floor. It was stark white, even after all these years, and had two faucets, one for the hot running water and one for the cold. A person had to be skilled to get the right mixture from each faucet to achieve a perfectly balanced temperature. Lying there in that warm water surrounded up to her neck by the honey and milk bubble bath soap she had packed, Merci knew she had made the right choice to come to the hotel instead of spending the night in the house. She rubbed her arms and legs slowly in wide circular motions, with just enough pressure to relax the knots in her tired muscles. She was stiff from the drive, but more from the stress.

Again without indication, her lips parted and she said out loud as if someone was listening, "Tomorrow is going to be crazy."

She paused, to see if the imaginary presence from back at the house had followed her around the corner, and was standing there waiting to agree. Talking to herself was not something she often did but had done twice in the last hour. Cincinnati was already trying to revert her back into someone she did not want to be.

"God help me," she mouthed through a breathless sigh. She lay there with thoughts sprinting through her mind at speeds close to record breaking.

Even with all that chatter in her head, Merci still managed to doze off. And in that very brief moment that lapses between consciousness and slumber, Merci was transported to the back seat of her grandparents Chevrolet. She was six years old and it was the first day of first grade. Her mother had walked her to school that morning, and her grandparents had picked her up. She would be staying with them each afternoon until after Charlotta got off work. This was to be the routine for the duration of the school year.

Merci's first day had been better than she could have hoped for. She was so excited. She and the little girl who lived next door to Merci had lucked-up on getting the same first-grade teacher and they had even been able to get desks right across the aisle from one another. Merci was busy telling her grandparents all about her day, while another narrative was taking form in the front seat of the car between Jorja Sweet and Grey.

"I told you to make her be quiet!" Merci had not even known that something was wrong until she heard the sound of the slap and her grandfather speaking in his gruff and demanding way.

Merci's head, which just minutes before was being twisted and turned about in the throw of her own 6-year-old glee, snapped forward, and she stared at the back of her grandfather's head in horror. The words that were spilling out like a water from a faucet just moments before were scared right out of her throat as if she had been the one who had been slapped.

"Sit back and shut up!" Jorja Sweet whispered sternly through gritting teeth. She never even turned around in the seat to look at Merci, but Merci knew she was being spoken to, and she obeyed for fear that her grandfather's hand would meet her jaw next. He'd never hit her, but she feared him all the same. He was mean even when he wasn't swinging.

Merci was shaken from her sleep, saved from her past for the second time that night by the sound of her cell phone ringing. She jumped so violently that she banged her knee on the freestanding, metal soap dish hanging over the side of the tub, which sent the soap and what seemed like a gallon of water careening clear across the bathroom floor.

"Shit!" she hissed, "Who could be calling me now?" Merci abandoned the bubble bath without even picking up the soap or getting the water up.

The bath, now just short of lukewarm and with just a few fleeting suds floating on the surface of the water, seemed suddenly unwelcoming and she darted uncovered and dripping wet to the bed, not even bothering to grab her towel from its hanging place on the hook on the back of the door. By the time she got to the bed and was able to reach for the phone on the nightstand, the phone had stopped ringing. Merci was immediately irritated at having missed the call despite her sprint and Olympic leap onto the bed to get to it, so instead of checking to see who'd called, Merci tended to her now throbbing knee.

The agitation with being in Cincinnati that she'd gotten in the tub to relieve now grew more intense than it had been before. She sat on the bed distractedly rubbing her banged up knee and trying to forget about the lucid dream of a horrible day that she hadn't thought about in years. Merci looked over at the phone and cursed the caller who'd had the nerve to hang up before she could make it across the room to answer. This night was getting worse by the minute, and Merci felt the pulling urge to be telepathically transported back to her run-a-way life in New York City.

So wound up, Merci didn't recognize at first how comfortable the bed was. But slowly she became cognizant of her surroundings. The room was very cozy, and the bed was so warm and cushiony that Merci couldn't resist the urge to snuggle herself into its bedding. She pulled back the huge, fluffy blanket and the soft, fresh sheets, climbed under them, slid to the center of the bed and plopped back onto the over-stuffed pillows, hoping to get lost in all the thickness. She didn't even care that her wet body was sticking to the cottony sheets. Merci only wanted the feeling that was making her skin crawl with frustration to go away. She lay buried in the middle of the bed, breathing breathlessly with her lids closed tight, as if she was trying to squeeze the dream she'd just had out of her brain through her eyes. Where had that dream come from? She hadn't remembered a scene from her childhood that vividly in years. Merci knew it was because she was there; she was home. And every angst she felt about tomorrow was intensified and reaffirmed.

Her phone began singing to her again, and Merci was starting to be sick of hearing her favorite singer's recorded voice. She made a mental note to change her ring tone in the morning. Grabbing her cell phone off the nightstand and fighting the urge to throw it across the room, she turned it off without even looking at the missed calls. She reached for the lamp sitting on the nightstand and twisted the knob until darkness filled the room and swallowed her up in solace. Naked and sweating, she fell into a restless sleep that snatched her back to the back seat of her grandparents Chevrolet every time she got close to anything that even remotely felt sound.

CHAPTER 6: THE TIES THAT BIND

The next morning, Merci awoke at 6:30 a.m. feeling like shit, as if she had slept on a bed of rocks instead of the plush king size bed she had spent the night in. Or better yet, she felt like she was mercilessly being subjected to the pounding of a hangover from a night of binge drinking. She lay in the bed surrounded by so many pillows that for a second she felt trapped inside the fortress of puffy walls; she couldn't see what was around her and lay there trying to remember where she was. By the white ceiling above she knew that she was not home. Her ceilings were painted a pistachio green.

Too tired of panic, Merci remained on her back, hidden in the pillows and shielded up to her chin by the over-stuffed blanket until her senses were restored. When she finally remembered that she was in Cincinnati in the Vernon Manor Hotel, she unavoidably also remembered what she was there for. She wanted to hide her head under the abundance of pillows and pretend like she was somewhere else, like in a gas chamber facing death! Anything but facing the next few days that lie ahead would have been an improvement.

When she attempted to lift her head over the mound of pillows she had awaken to found herself buried in, a sharp pain shot through her like a surge of electricity and immobilized her ascent. Again, she felt as if she had drank the night before, the kind of drinking done by party-goers who engage in mixing different kinds of liquor recklessly. Her head was pounding, her body was stiff and her stomach was in knots.

Knowing that relief came in the form of the Excedrin that she had packed in her toiletry bag, she rose, with more caution this time, and scooted to the bottom of the bed. She reached over its side and rummaged in her bag that lay on the floor below, until she heard the rattle of the pills. She grabbed the bottle, wrestled the top off, then popped three of the dry pills into her mouth and swallowed without any fluid but her own saliva to assist. Merci started to climb out of the bed, but decided to steal a few minutes more reclining and avoiding the inevitable, knowing that the events of the day could not begin without her.

A few minutes quickly turned into almost 30 minutes, as she lay there allowing the drugs in her system to take effect. It was not guilt that propelled her to a sitting position because the killer headache she'd lay there recovering from would not have let her move before it subsided anyway. Rather, she forcibly swung her legs off the high-standing bed because it had occurred to her that the sooner she started this journey, the sooner she'd see its end.

Besides, she thought as she made her way to the bathroom feeble step by slow and steady step, whether or not she decided to stay there, the cumbersome matter at hand was not likely to dissolve itself like the aspirin had done in her system, so she might as well get to it. These next three days would be the hardest test she'd ever have to endure, but she had decided before she left New York that no matter how much she hated having to do this, she would if it meant finally and permanently burying her mother and the life she never wanted to know in the first place.

By the time Merci had gotten dressed, it was a quarter to eight o'clock. The sun had grown from that pinkish-gold mix of colors that occurs just before the daytime glow to the wake-you-up burn of the golden yellow that sometimes peaked through blinds when they have not been fully closed the night before. Merci glanced out the window at absolutely nothing as she sat in the restaurant of the Inn and ate her breakfast, and in her dazing suddenly remembered that she had turned her phone off the night before.

She reached in her purse and pulled the cell phone out. Flipping its front up, she turned it on and saw the call displayed. The missed calls had been her Aunt Carmen and knowing her aunt, Merci was surprised to see only those two missed call. She swallowed the last of the muffin she had been pinching on, chased it with the last swig of her vanilla tea and dialed her aunt's number, waving the waiter over so she could pay her bill as the phone rang.

Carmen Samuel had been the only Samuel sister to marry, but it hadn't lasted long. His name was Hershel and Carmen had met him in college. Merci always believed that he'd left Carmen because like the rest of the Samuel offspring, she was unlovable. But Carmen was closed lipped about the what, the how, and the why of her marriage or her husband's abrupt departure from their marriage and from the city all together. Rumors were nothing new to her family, and like always, Carmen did the best she could to mask the ugly truth and replace it with cordial smiles and carefully chosen explanations for things she would never reveal.

Carmen picked up the phone on the third ring and without even saying hello demanded, "Where the hell have you been girl? Is that how New Yorkers do when they come into town, sneak in like bandits in the middle of night and then don't even think to call family to announce their safe arrival?"

Carmen's voice, though obviously agitated, was airy and delicate. Not really the whisper she'd grown up using, it had slightly more weight than that. Still it had never achieved an octave used by most people in normal conversation.

Merci hated being referred to as a girl, she was a woman and if Carmen had been anybody else but her aunt, she would have told her as much. Merci never passed up the chance to let the White girls at the publishing company where she worked know that for Black women the word "girl" was offensive and, therefore, not appropriate in reference to her, nor would it ever be tolerated.

To a small cast of the bunch who fancied themselves liberal and were always so quick to point out that they had Black friends and who actually had the nerve to ask why it was so offensive, Merci would reply with a response meant to be slightly more intimidating in the face of their courage. With the twist of her neck, usually reserved for use by gum popping, finger snapping girls from the hood, Merci would let them know that the word "girl" was indicative of the slave/owner relationship that had defined the unevenly divided ratio of power between Black women and White women 500 years before. The comment would usually end the conversation, as any talk of slavery will always make White people hurry to leave the room. Despite the rebellious attitude she harbored towards the word, Merci gritted her teeth and answered her aunt calmly, and ignored the twitching nerve in her neck.

"Aunt Carmen, it was such a long drive and I was tired when I made it in, I just really needed to get some rest."

"Well, I can understand that. I get tired too when I'm in a car for too long. Did you stay at the house?" Carmen's speech was a constant stream of random thoughts that she spoke as quickly as they entered her mind, which seldom allowed time for premeditation of what she was saying from statement to statement. Without pause Carmen continued.

"I called your cell phone last night. Did you listen to the message I left?"

Merci shook her head at the barrage of questions being spewed so quickly she hadn't had time to answer a single one of them. She had not even realized that a message had been left. She hadn't noticed the message indicator in the corner of the screen when she'd turned the phone on.

"I didn't get the message auntie. Like I said, I was tired. I didn't stay in the house. I couldn't"

"Oh child, I'm so sorry. I'm just going on and on and haven't even asked you how you were holding up." She sucked her teeth and apologized again. "You alright, child?"

"I'm here."

It was the only response that Merci could manage. It occurred to Merci that her aunt's habit of referring to women in adolescent terms was worse than she'd first assumed. She strained her brain to remember if her Aunt Carmen had always done that or if it was something she had acquired in her older age. Whichever it was, Merci decided she would let it go and try to move the conversation forward.

"Aunt Carmen, what was the message you left?"

"Well baby," again with the child synonyms, "We have to be over to the funeral home at 9:00 a.m. to view the body. Where are you staying? I hope not at some hotel. You know you can lay your head right here in my house."

Merci glanced at her watch, which read 8:04 a.m., ate the last strawberry in the fruit bowl she'd ordered, grabbed her purse and suitcase, and headed out of the eating area of the hotel.

"I'm at the Vernon Manor. It was closer last night than driving to your house."

She lied. The thought had never crossed her mind. Now on top of the aggravation her aunt was making her feel, she was also making her feel guilty. In an attempt to shake the feelings free from her conscious, Merci followed the lie with a half-hearted comment that did little to relieve her.

"Maybe I'll stay with you tonight. I hadn't really planned to spend money on accommodations while I was here."

The door keeper who'd moved to open the door as Merci approached the hotel's exit smiled widely at her and nodded his head in unison with his salutation of good morning. Merci smiled back as she passed through the opened door, unable to respond any more than that because her aunt Carmen was on the other end of the phone going a hundred miles a second about how ridiculous it would be for her to waste hard earned money for a hotel when she was at home with her family, especially with how expensive things were getting these days.

Merci cleared the awning covered, carpeted walkway that led from the hotel to the curb, and immediately needed to shield her eyes from the brightness of the early morning sun rays. She squinted at the light pouring over her like a golden shower, as her eyes needed time to adjust between the sun's brilliance and the unnatural inside light of electric bulbs. Walking to the parked car, head tilted to one side, cell phone squeezed between her shoulder and ear, purse dangling from the arm already being made uncomfortable by the position of her shoulder, rolling suitcase in tow and struggling to balance all three, she must have looked like a disoriented hermit being affected by the new feeling of the sun on her skin.

Further adding to the spectacle of the balancing act, Merci fought to get her arm up just far enough to get the sunglasses she held to the bridge of her nose. It never dawned on her to stop walking and readjust. There were really no clear thoughts in her head which was working for her at that moment, since the mindless state was also allowing her not to worry too much about how unprepared she really had been for this trip. Not being ready was a seldom occurrence for her because her strong will to stay in control always superseded.

If Merci had been firing on all cylinders she would have been more concerned with the thoughtlessness with which she was behaving. She had never even contemplated where she'd be staying while she was in Cincinnati. She had actually gotten on the road, had driven for eleven hours through the mountains of Pennsylvania stopping only two times to fill up, and never once thought about where she was going to stay.

She figured that she must have assumed that she would be able to get across the threshold of her grandparents home, inside the same walls that her mother's heart had given out in, and where she had lain for two days before being discovered. Charlotta Samuel had suffered the same fate as her father. Grey Samuel had also died in that house and also of a heart attack on a Sunday, in his bed alone and he had lain there all day until after Jorja, Charlotta, Carmen, Camille, and a 9-year-old Merci had come home from church, and had prepared and eaten dinner. He laid there defecating his last bowel movement out and until after the girls had gotten their evening baths, after Jorja Sweet had stretched out on the sofa to rest and the girls had settled in the middle of the living room floor to play jacks while waiting for bedtime. When Jorja Sweet had finally found him, rigor was setting in.

Merci interrupted her own thoughts as she found herself standing at the car without the key in her hand. Merci pushed her hand into the dangling hand bag, blindly shuffling through all the bullshit in her purse in search of the car keys.

"Aunt Carmen, are you still there?"

Carmen smacked her teeth. "Yes child, you the one that tuned out." Her aunt's octave increased ever so slightly, "You sure you up for this?"

"Do I have a choice?" Merci finally located the key in the very bottom of her Dooney and Burke drawstring, opened the back door of the car and, exasperated with her journey through the parking lot, flung her suitcase and toiletry bag in the backseat. She walked around to the driver's side, slid in behind the steering wheel and threw her purse over on the passenger side. As she settled down into the seat and wiped her sweaty forehead with the back of her hand, she heard Carmen smack her teeth again.

"You had a choice alright..." Carmen's voiced trailed off and then dramatically continued. "...could have decided not to be here indeed. But I think you chose right baby. I'm going to be there with you every single step of the way."

"That's sweet of you, Aunt Carmen. Do you want me to pick you up so that we can ride to the funeral home together?" Merci could feel herself relaxing under the promise of having someone there with her. She hadn't exactly known how things would go with the arrangements that still needed to be made.

"That would probably be best since we have to go to the house afterwards. We need to make sure it's clean and ready for the re-pass dinner tomorrow night."

Merci loved the way Carmen said "we", knowing that her aunt would not be able to do very much of the cleaning that needed to be done. Carmen had arthritis in her hips, bending and pulling and pushing were limited activities for her. Merci started the car and shifted into reverse to back out of the parking spot she had pulled into crookedly the night before.

"I'm on my way. I'm just going to blow, so come on out."

****

Merci and her Aunt Carmen arrived at the funeral home with just a few minutes to spare. It had taken longer than she thought to get there, or maybe she was just driving slowly. It wasn't like she was really eager to get there and thought she probably had paused a few extra unnecessary seconds at every light and stop sign. As they walked through the front door of Jordan and Jordan, she wondered if the mortician had put the right shade of foundation on her mother's face. Charlotta had always had the kind of complexion that was hard to match, golden with red tints underneath. Beige's didn't work and neither did bronze's. Merci remembered that as a child, Charlotta had complained about there never being any good foundations for black women on the market. Instead of running herself ragged looking for one, Charlotta opted to skip on the foundation and use a mixture of blushes to give her the glow she'd desired.

As they entered the parlor, a stout, long-faced woman approached them and with the most crooked smile Merci had ever seen, extended her hand in welcome.

"Good morning ladies. My name is Janice Carnes, funeral director here at Jordan and Jordan, and you must be the Samuel family. I can tell because you look just like the beautiful woman that was rolled to the viewing room an hour ago."

Merci did not take the woman's extended hand and felt a little awkward about the comment the woman had just made. She wasn't sure if what the woman said was intended as a compliment or an insult. Merci just stood there looking at this Ms. Janice Carnes in shaken disbelief and couldn't decide if she should be flattered because the woman thought her mother was beautiful even in death, or offended because the woman thought Merci looked like a corpse.

Carmen took the woman's hand, which had been left suspended in the space between Merci and Janice, "We are the Samuel family. We're running a little behind. I hope it is no inconvenience for you."

"None at all, my next appointment isn't for another hour." Janice Carnes' lopsided smile never wavered and she never seemed to notice that Merci had not returned her handshake. "Follow me. I am sure you all will be pleased with the work done on your loved one."

Merci thought the way Ms. Carnes spoke about the dead was eerie. But then again, how else could a funeral director bring life to her job? No pun intended. She and Carmen followed the funeral director through a corridor and then into a room that was cooler than the hallway they had just walked through. At the front of the room sat an ivory colored coffin with gold trim. Inside that coffin lay Charlotta's body. Merci didn't even realize that she had become frozen in her tracks. Carmen and Janice Carnes proceeded and stopped just inches from the coffin. Carmen immediately reached in and stroked Charlotta's cold, lifeless check.

"She is beautiful," Carmen said, still stroking Charlotta's face. "Merci, isn't she…" she stopped in mid-sentence realizing that Merci was not standing next to her. She spun around with a look of concern on her face. "I know this isn't easy Merci. But it isn't as bad as you think. You can do this baby, and I'm right here like I said I'd be."

Merci willed her legs to move and, finally standing in front of the coffin, glanced in to see the face of her mother looking rested and at peace; a state Merci seldom saw Charlotta in when she was a child. She wouldn't be as comfortable as her aunt had been, there was no way she'd be touching her mother's dead face. But it was true. Charlotta did look as beautiful as she had when she was alive.

Ms. Carnes broke the silence that had descended on the room "I take it that you all are pleased?"

"I think she looks like an angel." Carmen was beaming with pride or with nostalgia, Merci couldn't really tell. Merci didn't think she resembled anything about who Charlotta had been as much as an interpretation of what her Aunt Carmen wanted Charlotta to be.

Charlotta wore a white dress with a high, ruffled collar. Merci knew, without even asking, that her Aunt Carmen had chosen that outfit to bury her eldest sister in. Carmen always wanted Charlotta to be dainty, but Charlotta had too much girth to be dainty and she preferred kente colored, wrap dresses and head wraps, caire shell earrings and natural stone rings. The elaborately lacey dress wasn't something she thought Charlotta would have been caught dead in. Again, no pun intended. Merci thought her attire made Charlotta look like a member of the royal family or of the British parliament from centuries ago. She wondered what vintage Goodwill or costume store Carmen had gotten the dress from.

Charlotta's make-up was the only thing Merci thought came close to resemblance. It was not too heavy, and her beauty mole was as pronounced as it had always been. It even seemed a little more distinct than Merci remembered it to be. But her locs were gone and she knew her mother would not have permitted that either. Knowing that Carmen thought Charlotta's hair was a dirty, matted mess, Merci wasn't surprised that she decided to finally have her way since Charlotta could no longer defy her. The wig that replaced her twisted, crowning glory was a very stylish wig, but it wasn't Charlotta. Merci's first impulse was to ask her aunt why the hell she thought the wig would be a better idea than her mother's locks, but decided that there was nothing she could do about it now and she wasn't in the mood to argue about it.

As she stood there, staring into Charlotta's face, the face she'd always wished had shown love for her more openly, Merci felt tears begin to form in her eyes, and seeing this, her Aunt Carmen grabbed her hand, which dangled at her side as if it was Merci whose body was lifeless. A tear hung onto the bottom of her lid, but wouldn't drop. Still Merci felt like she needed to cry, like she was supposed to be wailing because after all, it was the woman that other's referred to as her mother lying in that coffin. As Merci squeezed her lids shut, trying to force the lone tear to loosen its stronghold, she wasn't sure if what she felt was sadness, relief or nausea. Truthfully, she just wanted this to be over and wondered how long a viewing was supposed to last.

Just as she thought she couldn't stand there any longer Ms. Carnes chimed in again. "So if Ms. Samuel's appearance is pleasing to you, we can retire to the office to go over the details of the service." She turned to leave the room without waiting for their response.

Merci and Carmen, still holding hands, followed Janice Carnes and her crooked smile back through the corridor and into a lavishly furnished office just off the parlor that they had previously stood in when they first arrived.

Ms. Carnes sat behind a mahogany desk that seemed like it belonged in an office on Wall Street rather than in the office of a funeral home. She adjusted her smile so that it was now twisted to the side opposite of where it had been fixed before, and motioned for Carmen and Merci to sit in the two high back leather chairs on the other side of the desk. It wasn't until they were seated that Carmen and Merci released their grip on each other's hands.

"Well then," the funeral director with the permanent smile began after Merci and Carmen settled into the plush cushion of the chairs, "I believe you all will be as satisfied with the program as you were with the results of our incredible stylist."

She handed the folded piece of paper to Merci and leaned back in her own high-backed leather chair with a slight arrogance that suggested there was no way the ladies could find displeasure with Jordan and Jordan's work.

Merci allowed her fingers to trace the frayed edges of the program, which had been intentionally designed that way and had become a popular design for funeral programs. The paper on which the program was printed was textured and soft to the touch like cotton, another popular design. It was ivory in color and had a gold ribbon draped over it near the fold to match the coffin Charlotta was laid out in. The letters were also gold and read *In Loving Memory*. And under the picture of Charlotta that had been chosen and was positioned in the middle of the page, was her name and the dates between her birth and her death.

The picture of Charlotta that had been chosen to grace the program was one Merci remembered being taken. It was a full body shot and had been taken when Charlotta had first returned from Jamaica. In the picture, she wore traditional Caribbean wrap around dress and a matching head wrap that allowed her locks to sprout through its top and fall over onto Charlotta's shoulder. Her smile held a warmness that lit up her eyes and she seemed soft and tranquil, unlike the stressed expression she had worn for so many years before her foreign hiatus; a stress that seemed to pinch her face and distort her natural beauty.

Apparently not the kind of woman who preferred silence, Ms. Carnes interrupted Merci's concentration on the photo. With an out-of-place pleasantness in her voice, she asked, "It's a lovely program, wouldn't you all agree?"

Carmen, who had been quiet for such a long time that her voice came out a little scratchy, agreed with Ms. Carnes, "It is very nice. The picture came out really well too. I thought it might be a little blurry since it was such an old photo."

"Never that!" Ms. Carnes recanted, "We had to touch it up a little, but thanks to the advancements of technology, we had no problems making it clear." Glancing at her watch and noticing that the hour she had reserved for the Samuel family was quickly dwindling down, she instructed the ladies to read over the program while she stepped out to prepare for her next appointment.

As soon as the door had closed, putting Ms. Carnes on the other side and back into the parlor, Carmen turned to Merci and said, "Your Aunt Camille came up with the design of the program and wrote the obituary. I think she did a good job. We decided the order of the service together."

Merci glanced over the obituary but couldn't find her voice as she read about the life Charlotta had led. She just nodded in agreement with what she had barely heard Carmen say. The obituary made it seem as if Charlotta had been a happy, well adjusted, Christian woman. It stated that Charlotta had been born the eldest and beloved daughter of Grey and Jorja Sweet Samuel and that she had given her life to God at an early age.

When it came to the part about Merci being her only and loving daughter, the words seemed to jump off the page and slap Merci across her cheek with a fierceness she had not expected. She so seldom referred to Charlotta as her mother and to herself as somebody's daughter that the words seemed foreign to her. Still, Merci continued to read, and felt strangely betrayed when at the end of the paragraph about her, nothing had been mentioned about who her father was. Merci's eye began to twitch and the back of her neck suddenly became tight and warm. She was finally just tired of the secrets.

Sensing that Merci was slightly agitated and knowing exactly why, Carmen rushed to explain. "I know you didn't think we'd write the truth."

"Why not?" Merci continued to stare at the program as if looking for answers on its pages to questions she'd been asking all her life. "It's not like everybody doesn't already know how twisted our family really is."

Merci could feel the anger start to swell up in her body. It was an anger that had grown roots in her soul, despite the fact that Merci had always tried to pretend like she was no longer angry about her past.

"Now listen, Merci," It was the first time since she'd first spoken with her aunt that morning that she had not referred to her as a girl, a child or a baby, "We've all suffered long enough. And God knows Charlotta suffered enough for all of us, so much so that she willingly released her handle on reality and floated through life like some gypsy woman who claimed to have healing powers in her hands and between her legs. There is no reason for us to send her to her final resting place followed by the ugliness of her life. Doesn't she deserve some happiness in death?"

"Maybe you've forgotten, Aunt Carmen," Merci snapped her head around to look at her aunt who had been staring at her while Merci stared at the obituary, "But that woman lying in that back room looking like a plastic Barbie doll lived more in her truth than any one of us before she died, or at least figured out that none of it was her fault and found some part of herself to love.

Merci shifted her entire body towards her aunt to get in a better position for the stare down Carmen had engaged her in, and continued.

"She was smart enough to get away and seek some kind of understanding, and if nothing some peace of mind. That's what her hiatus in Jamaica was all about. She had to separate herself from the past to make some kind of future for herself. You're just mad because you didn't have the same kind of courage. You always wanted her to be somebody else, which is obvious by the shit you chose for her to be buried in!" Merci spat the words at her aunt with a harshness she could not control.

"No,'" Carmen retorted with as much fierceness as she could force, trying to match the fever, the passion in Merci's words, "What Jamaica was about for Charlotta was running away. You know all about that, don't you?"

Merci reared her head back and laughed the kind of laugh that seemed to say, *I'll be damned!* She couldn't believe her aunt would have the nerve to go there with her! Merci leaned closer to Carmen.

"For your information, I did not run away, I flew. That's right! I got the hell up out of here. If I acquired nothing from my mother's detached way of loving me, I surely learned how to love from a distance and do what I need to do to keep myself sane. I can't wait for this whole ordeal to be over so

I can get the hell out of this infected environment. You and Aunt Camille are so immersed in the thick of it that you still talk like you're afraid to let somebody hear you and she can't even admit that she's slowly deteriorating in the acid of her anger."

The words Merci threw like ninja knives at her aunt were so hurtful Carmen was almost wincing with each precise blow. She was pissed too, but her voice never wavered from its breath-filled wisps, even as Merci pointed out the programmed conduct to her.

"If you believe Charlotta resolved all the issues in her life by allowing some jungle guru to lay hands on her, then you are as unstable as she was. She was no more in touch with herself, her family or with reality after she returned than she was before she *ran* away. She just stopped feeling guilty about being aloof. You call it freedom and peace of mind. I call it selfishness. She had no right to come back here and live in that house knowing that Camille and I were against it! She just didn't give a damn. And the continuous flow of men, in and out, doing only God knows what while they were there..." Carmen's voice was shaking. It blew at Mercy like a passing wind.

"Where else was she going to go?" "Merci was screaming now, "You weren't so quick to open your home to her as you did to me this morning. That damn house was just here, empty, closed up, binding its ghosts inside. What did you think, that as long as the front door never opened again you could lock the truth away?'"

"I tried to let her stay with me, it just didn't work,'" Carmen tried to regress. "Your mother's talking, constantly talking, is what wore her welcome out. Can you imagine? She wanted to reminisce about things. I couldn't have it, not in my house! He was dead, mama was dead, it was over and I found no good in talking about it."

"And you think we're the only ones running somewhere? Wow, you sure are delusional!" Merci had taken on some self-righteous attitude, defending the care-free behavior that Charlotta had acquired to replace her distant approach to life; both of which kept her isolated her from her sisters and from Merci. That was her coping mechanism and it was no different than the survival tools either of her aunts or herself had picked up along the way.

Carmen, however, seemed hell-bent on restoring what was left of the family's fragile reputation by pretending it didn't happen at all and hadn't left such destruction in its aftermath. Camille protected herself from it with a wall of anger, a slew of prescription drugs and ridiculous amounts of weed, and casually random lesbian lovers. And Merci hid behind a façade of beauty, in a shallow prison that she could escape from but had become too comfortable in. She locked herself away from love as if it were some kind of plague from which she needed to be quarantined, never letting anyone in, living an elusive life with a made-up past far away from where she had come from, and giving only of herself physically to men. She was selective in her choosing but took full advantage of her popularity with the opposite sex, knowing that she had the assets to have a plethora to choose from and the hardened interior enough to walk away when things were getting too heavy; and things always did.

Merci was not finished yet, "And the fact that you decided to dress her up like some 1930's Sunday school teacher instead of leaving her locks alone and putting her in an outfit that she would have worn in her real life is proof that you are as selfish and self-absorbed as you are always saying that she was, as any of us are."

"Watch your tone with me!" Carmen snapped, her feelings, having already been crushed, were now being grinded under the heavy boot of her niece's tirade and by the accusation that she and her sister had abandoned Charlotta.

"Yeah, okay, Aunt Carmen, I'll watch my tone as soon as you accept the truth. Charlotta wasn't perfect, but none of us ever will be because your father was a sick, sick man, and he is my father too! I'm your niece and your sister!"

It's not like Merci ever wanted to claim him, but for some reason, here she was asserting her possession over Grey Samuel like he was some kind of prize to be won. Her voice had risen to an octave that seemed to bounce off the walls of the office and land in Carmen's lap.

Carmen shook with annoyance but never raised her voice beyond the soft lilt that it had always been. "What would be the point of dragging this family any further into the pits of hell? For your information Merci, we all moved on the best way we could, your mother's way just never cared how she affected anyone else. She thought her hurt was somehow worse, her wounds somehow deeper, than mine, than Camille's, even more than mama's pain. And you were the reason she thought that. You were her proof that she had it worse than anyone else. But she's gone now and I am ready to let it go, so should you."

"I need to let it go, but Aunt Camille won't even acknowledge that her last name is Samuel?" Merci was being sarcastic now, and somewhat cruel. Camille had long ago changed her last name to Patterson, which was Jorja Sweet's maiden name. Merci had called her Aunt Camille a coward then, and felt as strongly about it now as when she had first learned of her aunt's decision.

"I think you need to calm down baby." Carmen had resorted back to the use of the child-like adjectives again, which signaled her white flag surrender. She reached over to pat Merci's hand that was resting on the arm of the chair "Let's just get out of here. I think the atmosphere in here is starting to get to both of us." Carmen's annoyance had subsided, but she was feeling jumpy and the cushioned, leather chair was starting to feel like led under her rear end.

Merci stood up and turned to leave, still feeling heated and ready to explode. But with who or what was she angry about and why she had gotten so upset was unclear to her. She wrestled with why not being called a product of incest in Charlotta's obituary even bothered her at all? This was, after all, supposed to be about Charlotta, not about her. But could something be about Charlotta and not be about her, about all the Samuel women, Josephine, Jorja Sweet, Carmen and Camille?

When she opened the door of the office, Ms. Carnes stood in the corridor with her mouth hanging open. It was obvious that she had heard the details of the squabble between Merci and Carmen, or at least Merci's part of the conversation since she was the only one screaming. Merci brushed past her without saying a word, and Ms. Carnes just looked at Carmen in disbelief, and what appeared to be pity.

"Is there something I can do to help you all?" Ms Carnes didn't know what else to say. She stood there as if frozen to the floor, feeling helpless and awkward.

"No, everything is fine. The program looks great.

We'll be here tomorrow at 11:00 a.m., as scheduled. Do you need anything else from us at this time?" Carmen's thoughts started spilling out in run-on sentences again, as this was her normal state of conversation.

Ms. Carnes stuttered her response, "Uh, no. The wake will begin promptly at 11:00 a.m. The family car will be at the house to pick you all up no later than 10:15. Is that okay?"

"We'll be ready. Thanks for everything. I'm sure it will be a lovely service."

Carmen moved passed Ms. Carnes, whose smile had finally faded, and rushed to catch up with Merci. Merci was sitting in the car, sweating like a run-a-way slave when Carmen slid into the passenger seat. They sat in silence for a few minutes. Carmen finally broke the silence.

"Please start the car and role the windows down baby. I'm going to melt into the seat," she said as she leaned forward to look at the blazing sun coming through the windshield like a high-powered laser.

Merci turned the key in the ignition and hit the power buttons to activate their windows. Without looking at her aunt, she shifted the car into drive and sped out of the parking lot of Jordan and Jordan at break-neck speed, and pushed down Gilbert Avenue towards her old neighborhood. The thoughts that were running through her mind were moving at speeds she couldn't control or decipher. She drove the few miles to Corryville in silence and frustration. She couldn't figure out where her outburst had come from, and she couldn't explain why she had gotten so mad. Her head was starting to hurt again and all she wanted to do was find a place to lay down and drown in her tears.

Merci had somehow made it back to Corryville and to the Samuel house, although she couldn't recall even seeing the streets, the traffic lights or any of the people on the streets between the funeral home and their final destination. When the car came to a halt in the driveway of the house, again the two ladies sat in silence. Carmen decided she wouldn't try to talk to Merci at that moment because she was sure Merci wouldn't hear her anyway. She just got out of the car and went into the house, leaving Merci sitting in the car alone.

And Merci finally cried; cried for all the years she hadn't. She cried for Charlotta, lying dead in an ivory colored casket that she'd soon be spending the rest of eternity in; ashes to ashes, dust to dust. She cried for her family, a group of women who never found the love of a man to comfort them. She cried for her grandmother, Jorja Sweet, who died with the guilt of her decisions weighing heavy on her heart. She cried for herself because she knew that the tears that rolled down her cheeks in droves would never be enough to cleanse her dirty little secret from her memory. She cried for Grey Samuel, for his illness, for his meanness, for his soul; a soul she knew would be tortured in hell for as long as the earth spun on its axis.

CHAPTER 7: UP CLOSE AND PERSONAL

Merci's tears eventually dried up and she somehow found the strength to get out of the car. With shaky nerves and unstable legs, she stood on the porch of the Samuel family house reliving the same halting fear she had experienced the night before. Determined not to be beaten Merci finally got up the nerve to push open the door and step into her past.

The house looked just like it did when Merci was a child and she was instantly transported back there. Standing there in the entrance way, she felt four years old again and overwhelmed with a tremendous sadness; it was a sadness that would come over her every time she entered her grandparents' house as a little girl, a sadness she couldn't understand then because she did not know that it had less to do with her than it did to do with the energy that lived and breathed there, always circulating through the stale and weighted air between its walls.

Though they were not, the furniture and the curtains all seemed to be the same, but the all-consuming space had not changed which made the memories of the days she had spent there as real today as they had been actual two decades ago. The foyer was speckled with splotches of light that shown through the small window to the left of the front door. The wood of the staircase that led up to the second floor of the house was still worn, displaying a dullness that Jorja Sweet could never make shine despite the constant care she'd given to them.

To the left of the front foyer was the dining room and on the other side of the dining room was a kitchen big enough to cook a meal for an army. To the right of the foyer was the living room, and on the other side of it, a den. A guest bathroom sat down the hall from the den, and in the parallel hallway on the left side of the staircase was a corridor that led to the sunroom that Grey Samuel had insisted on adding on. No one understood the persistence about the closed in back porch. But just as the one on his father's house where he'd gone to hide as a child from his mother's sins, the sun room connected to the Samuel house was where he went to hide from his sins against his own children.

After thoroughly examining the house, Merci looked back to her left and focused her attention on her Aunt Carmen who sat at the dining room table with her head resting in the cup of her left hand. She held her cell phone to her ear with her free hand. As Merci walked into the dining room she came into hearing range of her Aunt Carmen on the phone with whom Merci assumed was her Aunt Camille.

"When are you coming this way? We are really going to need your help getting this house together. Charlotta must have never cleaned because there is so much dust on the floors my feet are leaving tracks."

Carmen glanced at Merci just as she plopped into the chair on the opposite end of the table, but said nothing to acknowledge that she was there. Unable to judge whether or not Merci was in a better mood, Carmen kept her attention on her sister's voice.

Camille was going on and on about how she had no intentions on spending her day cleaning and cooking. Growing weary of Camille's complaining, Carmen massaged her temples, trying to relieve the tension that was slowly developing into a headache. Her last nerve had been worked and she was getting fed up with her sister's and her niece's bad moods. She huffed at Camille's ranting, but waited for her to finish.

"You act as if I'm jumping for joy!" Carmen took the opportunity to jump in when the need to inhale caused Camille to pause. "But the house has to be cleaned and dinner has to be prepared for the re-pass."

"And that's my problem?" Camille was determined to be difficult even though she had promised to help.

"It's no one's problem, Camille. But I see you just want to be ugly today. I don't need it, so don't come today and don't show up tomorrow. I really don't care anymore. If no one else is going to give a damn, why should I?" Carmen's use of profanity let Merci know that her aunt had reached her limit because the use of expletives was something she was not used to hearing from the mouth of her usually holy aunt.

"I didn't say I wasn't coming!" Her Aunt Camille was screaming so loud that Merci could hear her as clearly as if it was her ear instead of Carmen's that had been violated with Camille's shrill. "I just don't plan to be there all day!"

Carmen pushed back some of her frustration and forced her ever-present calmness to resurface. "Get here when you can. I'm hanging up before I lose any more of my religion."

She removed the phone from her ear and pressed the end call button before Camille could retort. Merci could barely look at her aunt. She knew that Carmen's frustration was directed at her attitude too, not just at her Aunt Camille. Searching her mind for the words to ease the ruffled feathers she had helped to dishevel, Merci cleared her throat in preparation of an apology.

But before the words could find their way to the air between them, Carmen sighed heavily and said, "Guess we better get started."

She held her gaze on her niece waiting to see if her mood had improved. She wanted to be angry with Merci for her tantrum, but understood where her anger was coming from. Merci finally met her aunt's eyes and without words, both women understood that there was no need for an apology.

Merci smiled weakly and reached across the table to take her aunt's hand. The pair of them sat quietly for a few more seconds and then, almost simultaneously, pushed themselves back from the table and got to work. Very few words were being passed between them as they dusted and swept and wiped away months old dirt from every surface in the house. Each consumed by her own thoughts, her own memories, her own struggles.

Merci found herself in the master bedroom, redressing the same bed her grandparents had shared so long ago, the same bed Grey Samuel had died in when she was nine years old, the same bed Charlotta had done who knows what in for the last 10 years. She had died there too. It seemed disgusting to Merci that her mother did not get a new bed when she moved into the house. Merci had questioned hundreds of time how Charlotta could have slept in the bed her father had taken his last breath in, let alone in the same house she had lost her innocence in and had known so much pain in. But since there were no answers to those questions, Merci realized how senseless they were to ponder.

As she slipped the last pillowcase over a flattened pillow, her thoughts fell on the eulogy she was supposed to deliver tomorrow and the words she had not yet found to say. Without warning, anxiety began to creep along her spine and gather in an awful knot at the nape of neck, making her body hot and tense. Merci rubbed her neck and pressed hard on the area where most of the tightness could be felt. The knot that had gathered started to dissipate, but only caused her brain to tingle with agitation. Merci's breathing became labored and it felt as if she would lose consciousness if she could not summons her composure.

Just as she was reaching for her chest, trying to steady the intensity she felt there, her Aunt Carmen entered the room and began chattering without even noticing the sweat glistening on Merci's temple, or the look of fret on her face.

"Merci, I made a grocery list of things we will need to prepare the re-pass meal. Your Aunt Camille just called and is on her way. Let her clean up the bathrooms since she hasn't been here for the rest of the torturous labor."

Carmen was back to her usually talkative self, tumbling through her words as if she'd forget them if she couldn't get them out in a rush. "Is it okay if I use your car to go to the grocery store?"

Grateful for the interruption and for not having to get back in her friend's cramped car to drive her aunt to the grocery store, Merci's nervousness retreated and she managed a response that hid the state of madness she had just come so close to.

"The keys are in my purse hanging on the dining room chair I was sitting in." She wiped her brow and wanting not to be left alone so quickly, she added, "What are you picking up at the store?"

Merci's feigned interest went unnoticed as Carmen rambled on, "Well, I've asked people who plan to attend the re-pass to bring a side dish of their liking. I'm going to take care of the meat and dessert. Roast beef, baked chicken, and fried whiting. I figure those are enough choices. I'm also going to pick up ingredients for a peach and pear cobbler, a chess pie, a strawberry cheesecake, a red velvet cake and a German chocolate cake. What do you think?"

"I think you've gone overboard on the dessert, but it all sounds so good I can't figure out which one I'm going to eat first!" Merci was almost salivating. Sweets were her weakness and she fondly recalled, in that instance, how good her aunt was at creating some of the most delectable treats a tongue could taste. Carmen's red velvet cake was inarguably the best in the city. Most people who fancied themselves pros at making the richly decadent cake made it with only two layers, but her Aunt Carmen's version stood three layers tall and the cream cheese icing was made from scratch.

"Well, I love baking, you know that." Carmen was smiling with pride, knowing that everyone she knew loved her baking too. And with that, she was floating out of the room on a sugar-high.

Merci listened to the heal of her aunt's shoes click down the wooden steps and heard the front door squeak open and slam shut. She was alone in the house and alone with her thoughts again. Normally, solitude was comfortable for Merci. But standing there in that house, she felt haunted and momentarily regretted not going with Carmen to the grocery store. She hoped her Aunt Camille would hurry up and get there.

Merci inhaled deeply, laid the pillow neatly in its place, and left the bedroom. Walking just a few paces to her left, she stood at the threshold of the second bedroom that her Aunt Carmen and Aunt Camille used to share as children. From where she stood, she could see the dust stacked on the dresser in the far corner of the room without even stepping inside. The rest of the room seemed to be in order and grateful for that, Merci decided that she would only need to dust and vacuum in there.

Moving quickly through that task, Merci's last stop was the room directly across the hallway. It used to be Charlotta's bedroom. Being the oldest girl had its privileges because Charlotta had never had to share that space with either of her sisters. Charlotta's room was about 20 feet from and on the same side of the hallway as the bathroom, which Merci was glad she wouldn't have to clean. Merci could not remember the last time she had so much cleaning to do. Her own apartment back in Harlem never required much more than a quick cleanup because she seldom had visitors to impress. Karissa was her most frequent visitor and she never seemed to care about dust or furniture with untidy surfaces.

So consumed in her thoughts, Merci entered her mother's childhood bedroom without pause or contemplation of what awaited her inside. The air in the room was stiff, having not been inhabited for so many years. Unlike Carmen's and Camille's bedroom, the door to Charlotta's room stayed closed and the heavy drapes that hung at the small window were tightly closed, which only intensified the urge to hurl that had suddenly gripped Merci at the throat.

The things that Merci normally found comfort in like closed window shades and doors and spending time alone were now causing her tremendous distress. Being in Cincinnati was gradually becoming a cross she wished she had never decided to pick up. Feeling smothered, Merci labored through the dusting and vacuuming in Charlotta's old room and no matter how hard she fought, images of episodes that she imagined had occurred there ran rampant through her mind. She was suddenly exhausted and felt compelled to rest. As if in some kind of trance, Merci switched the vacuum off and lay across the bed's width. If she had been in a conscious mind-state, there was no way she would have ever crawled into her mother's girlhood bed; the same bed where the dirty deed of incestuous conception had taken place.

Merci's eyelids slid down over her pupils against her will and she nodded into a half-slumber that invited scenes she had never personally witnessed to creep in. In her dream-like state, Merci became her 15-year-old mother, curled up in a tight ball under the blanket shivering and afraid. In a flash, Grey Samuel was standing at her side and staring down upon his daughter in lust. Charlotta never looked up to meet his gaze, and she didn't need to see his eyes to know that he was getting ready to slide in next to her. His warm hands explored her body in slow, almost reassuring strokes as if he were promising not to hurt her. But hurt was inevitable.

In her sleep, Merci could feel his touch. She tossed around on the bed trying to wake herself from the dream but couldn't find her way back to the here and now. Of all the frightening dreams she had ever had, this was the worst. She was reliving an encounter as if she was Charlotta, and even though she knew she was asleep, it all felt so real.

She heard his voice and felt his whisper on her neck, "Daddy missed you baby girl."

He sounded like every pervert Merci had ever seen on her favorite cop show, Law and Order Special Victims Unit. Grey's hands were on her breast now, squeezing and pinching her nipples between his fingertips. She felt herself being rolled over, the grip of his rough palm around one and the descent of the tip of his tongue come down on the other nipple, and then the pain from his teeth biting down, forcing his erection from the stimuli. Merci cried out from the dream and again tried to shake herself from the awful nightmare, but to no avail.

His hand slid down her torso, over her belly, and into her mound of puffy pubic hair. He lingered there, running his fingers through the softness of the strands while a moan of desire escaped from his throat in a husky, mannish sound that made Merci shiver. It was as if she and Charlotta were one. The little girl in the dream had her mother's face, but it was Merci's body that lay trapped in the bed, pinned under the weight of Grey's heavy arm.

Having grown tired of playing just outside of her softness and wanting to experience the wetness he had coerced between her thighs, she could feel Grey's fingers part the lips of her own vagina and flick her clitoris with his middle finger. She gasped as he plunged two fingers into her fleshy softness, and stretched her apart as he jabbed in and out scraping her walls with his jagged nails.

She felt her body respond, betraying her and bringing forth a sticky moisture that let Grey know she was ready to be entered. So real was the weight of his body as he mounted her and pushed her knees apart, exposing the sweet smell of juices that mocked the true feelings of disgust she was choking on.

Merci could smell his Old Spice cologne overwhelm her nostrils and further suffocate her senses. Merci could feel the tears that slid down her own neck and met the pillow under her own head. She felt every bit of the rape occurring but could also clearly see the scene from a vantage point that suggested she was floating above it.

And then, in a frenzied rush, he was inside of her, pumping hard and fast, grunting and slobbering like the crazed rapist that he was. Charlotta's whimpers threatened to distract him, so he covered her mouth with his palm and kept right on pumping. Her bodily functions continued to be disloyal to her, responding with a waterfall of wetness and making Grey grow harder in between her walls. He grabbed her thighs, Merci's thighs, and pushed them back until they lay against her stomach, better angling his position so that his entire member could get inside.

It was Merci's body that lay there, lifeless and petrified to do anything but allow him to finish, but the scared look of Charlotta's face grew more intense with every stroke. As Grey reached climax, he wrapped his big hands around her neck and applied enough pressure to make her gasp. He wasn't trying to choke her as much as trying to stifle any movement that would interrupt his orgasm. He exploded inside of Merci with a pulsing vibration of a man fully satisfied, and as quickly as he had entered her room, he was gone, leaving her lying there with his juices running out of her vagina and down in between her butt cheeks. Merci felt herself pull the covers back up over her body and could see the steady stream of silent tears running down Charlotta's cheeks.

Merci had had many a dream in her lifetime, but this was the realest dream she could remember ever suffering through. Why had it felt like her own body being violated when it was her mother's sorrowful eyes that reflected the agony and the shame of being her father's concubine? Although the dream had ended, Merci remained asleep and stopped fighting the need to wake up. And that's how Camille found her, sprawled across the bed with dried tears stained onto her face as if they had been painted there.

****

Camille stood in the door of the bedroom, watching her niece sleep. It had been years since she'd seen Merci and she was a little surprised at how much she looked like Charlotta and Grey. Her complexion was the perfect blend between Grey's mocha colored skin and Charlotta's reddish, hazel hue. She had Charlotta's full lips and Grey's thick, wavy hair. Camille felt a wave of nausea begin to spread through her body and overwhelm her senses; it was like staring at the dead.

Merci lay perfectly still and her breath was calm and even, but from the streaks of dried tears on her face, Camille knew that her slumber was anything but peaceful. Choosing not to disturb her and trying to regain some composure, Camille backed out of the room and softly closed the door. Not sure what work was left to be done, Camille tip-toed through the house peeking into every room as if she was afraid to disturb more than her niece.

It had been years since Camille had been inside of her childhood home. In recent years, she had only gone as far as driving past on those sleepless nights when she needed to get close to her past in hopes of gaining some kind of understanding. The day she moved out, she vowed never to step foot across its threshold, and she held to that promise like it was her only source of sanity. She was the most stubborn and hateful of the sisters and there were times when she didn't understand her own emotions, but she felt entitled to her hatred and her self-imposed isolation.

Without warning, Camille began to feel sick. Sweat poured from her forehead and down her neck and back. Her chest became tight and she was sure she was about to lose her footing. Needing to sit before she fell, she made her way down the stairs, staggering but upright. She made it to the living room and collapsed on the sofa. The pine smell of furniture polish invaded her senses, increasing the weakness that had overcome her. There was no way she could stay here and her only thought was getting the hell out of that house. Camille summoned enough strength to push herself up and off the sofa. She stumbled to the front door and ran out without closing it behind her. Her descent off the porch was clumsy and uncoordinated, but she made it back to her car unscathed. The taillights of her Toyota Avalon zoomed out of sight and Camille never looked back.

CHAPTER 8: MEMORIES THAT LIVE LIKE PEOPLE DO

After spending six hours cooking and cleaning, Carmen was exhausted. She had only done the light cleaning, dusting and fluffing the sofa pillows, but had done the bulk of the cooking. Carmen insisted that all Merci do to contribute to the meal was season the meat since Merci had had to do the hard cleaning; vacuuming the furniture and carpeted floors in the living room and bedrooms, sweeping and mopping the tile floors in the kitchen and in the bathrooms, waxing the wood floors in the foyer, dining room, and the upstairs hallway, and giving the wood steps a heaping coat of Murphy's Oil in hopes to restore a shine that never lasted longer than the hour after the shining. Merci had also ended up cleaning the upstairs and downstairs bathrooms since it didn't seem that Camille had.

The work was almost over and Carmen felt sure that it had been split fairly between the two of them. It meant so much to her that everything be fair, that she played her part in making things just right. Standing in the kitchen looking at the spread that lay before her, she felt satisfied. Baking was her release, and today she had baked enough to relieve all the tension that the day began with. Her legs tingled, her hips were stiff and her feet hurt, but all in all, the day was not a waste and she was pleased with the combined effort put forth by herself and her niece. She could not remember one time when the women in her family had actually worked together to do something good, and she was proud.

Carmen was the middle child. She'd never been the oldest or the baby of the family, which always made her second to either of the two. So being sacrificial came natural for her. It was, as it is for most middle children, how she asserted an identity for herself and it gave her a distinction in the family's core. Charlotta was the chosen, Camille was the scapegoat and she was the pretender. Carmen needed things to look right even if there was madness in the midst, and she did what she could to keep the order.

She'd listen without saying a word and agreed while Camille ranted and raved about how messed up they all were. She'd call Charlotta some Sundays before going to church just to make sure she hadn't taken ill or been raped by one of the strange men she "serviced" in their parent's bed. She made herself available to her niece the few times Merci had called on her to talk her through some threatening breakdown, despite the miles between them and having only her words over a phone wire to get through, she always tried to make things better for everyone she loved. It was her self-imposed duty to protect her family's name and never ever admit how bad it really was. She fixed things, protected images, tried to talk sense into people. If everything looked good, people would believe that it was good.

Carmen could hear Merci moving about the house,

busying herself with doing one final walk through, inspecting her day's work and making sure all the lights were turned off. She began wrapping up the food and was arranging the dishes in the refrigerator just as Merci entered the kitchen.

"Are we about finished here?" Merci stood in the doorway stretching and yawning, she sounded as tired as Carmen felt. Both were grateful to see the work coming to an end. Neither spoke about Camille's obvious arrival and disappearance before they even saw her face. And neither of them called her to find out what had caused her to come and leave so abruptly that she couldn't manage to close the front door.

The first thing that crossed Carmen's mind when she returned from the grocery store to find the front door of her parent's house sitting wide open was the question her mother, Jorja Sweet, used to ask her or her sisters when one of them would do the same thing on their way out to play in the front yard, "Do you think we live in a barn?" Followed by a direct demand to, "Close the damn door."

"I believe we are," Carmen smiled and approached her niece. She had an urge to hug Merci and the feeling confused her. They had never been an affectionate group of women, having been stripped of that natural human expression early in life. It had being replaced by distrust and fear of getting too close and by the anger that grew from being able to do nothing to change this most undesirable trait about each of them.

Instead of embracing Merci, Carmen opted to pat her on the shoulder and could only extend a barely audible, "Let's go."

Both women exited the house and walked into the late evening air. Dusk had begun to settle overhead bringing the end of the day into existence and foreshadowing the much needed rest that they hoped would be in store for them.

Carmen's legs had never been so happy to rest. Easing into the front seat of the car, she allowed her muscles to relax and she all but dissolved into the cushion of the seat. She yawned so hard that her eyes watered and she struggled to stay focused. Losing the battle, she rested her head on the headrest and closed her eyes.

It seemed like only minutes had passed before Merci pulled up in front of the three-bedroom cottage-style home that her aunt lived in alone. Anxious to get in the house and see the end of this day, Carmen shook off her exhaustion momentarily and scurried from the car. She grabbed Merci's jacket and toiletry bag from the back seat while Merci dragged her suitcase from the trunk. They looked like one ragged pair; Merci's coal black hair had fallen loose from the ponytail she had it pulled back into, the renegade strands lay flat against her forehead and her crumbled, musty clothing looked as if she had thrown them on right out of the dirty clothes basket, and Carmen was limping up the walkway, stepping down gingerly on her sore feet and shifting from side to side to avoid putting too much pressure on either hip.

By the time Carmen got Merci settled in the guest room and retired to her own quarters, the feeling of exhaustion had returned with a fierce intent to lay her flat, and Carmen couldn't even manage to get her bra, her socks, or her camisole off. She threw herself on her bed partially undressed and fell asleep almost immediately. But floating on the emotions of her day, her sleep would not invite her into the peace of happy dreams she'd hoped for.

A clear image of Herschel, the one and only man who had ever loved her, appeared behind her closed lids as if a photo had been glued there. He looked so handsome with his neatly cropped two inch afro, perfectly trimmed mustache and satin textured mahogany complexion, standing there beside her at the altar in the charcoal grey suit he had picked out himself for their special day.

She remembered that his eyes held the look of love in them, but when Carmen recalled her own reflection, standing there in the white, lacey contraption that her mother had insisted upon with the excessively tight bodice that had stills stiff enough to cut into her sides, her eyes were sad and her disposition was anything but loving. And the only person on her mind was her mother and how she had chosen that ugly dress just to spite her because she so disapproved of Carmen's getting married right out of college instead of waiting until she had something of her own getting in this world; something other than a man.

Carmen understood why her mother felt that way, considering the man she had married. But she was marrying Herschel Kellogg, not Grey Samuel, and Herschel was a stable young man with clear direction about his future as a pharmacist. And since she had spent the last four years at University of Maryland – Eastern Shore piddling through a liberal arts program that amounted to a Bachelor's Degree in absolutely nothing, her best option was to find a man who could take care of her if she lost a few jobs along the way because all she was going to have was a job and not a career like him. She never aspired to be anything but a helpmate, tending to everybody else's misery and trying to make everybody else happy had been all she'd ever done, all she'd ever wanted to do.

And besides, he loved her, and he was a man whom by all accounts she should have been able to give her love to. He adored her, he worked hard, he was God-fearing and loyal, and no woman ever laid eyes on him without voicing her approval of his good looks. And he chose her in all of her quiet awkwardness. Of all the women on campus he could have had and who vied for his attention every chance they were granted, Herschel Kellogg desired her, the way a man was supposed to long for a woman, for his woman. But she was afraid and inhibited and had never had sex with anyone else but her father. She didn't know what she was supposed to feel or what she was supposed to say when Herschel prepared to enter her for the first time.

She had practiced over and over again in the months leading up to the wedding, rehearsed at night in the silence of the small apartment she rented just off campus, saying sexy phrases out loud and panting to see if she sounded believable to herself. She didn't, and the realization that she might not be able to have a normal sex life would send her into convulsing and uncontrollable sobs that would not relent until she would finally fall asleep.

Carmen remembered the exact number of times that her father had torn at the innocence of her barely formed pubescent body; twelve times before Charlotta had gotten pregnant, before the shame of his incestuous lust manifested in the form of a bastard seed causing him to lose his appetite for any kind of carnal pleasure.

When he would enter the room she and Camille shared, he'd first make sure that Camille was asleep and then ease up behind Carmen, calling her his meek one, or his timid little pussycat. He preferred to take her from behind so he would not have to see the sad blankness in her eyes. Carmen would lie between the mattress and his solid frame, face turned to one side and cheek pressed into the pillow, humming a song in her head to drown out his mutterings. The humming got on his nerve sometimes, so he'd bite her ear and tell her to call him Daddy Grey while he humped, up and down on her teenage body, and she'd mumble the name mindlessly to the rhythm of the constant tune in her head. The abuse lasted for a year and she was just turning 13-years-old the last time he did his business with her, and she had never had sex with any other man since then.

Sometimes, on nights when she was not the daughter he had chosen to pay his late night visit to, she'd wonder what he said to Charlotta when she had her private time with daddy. What was his pet name for her? Neither of them ever talked about what he did with the other.

At that time, Camille wasn't old enough for intercourse yet, so there were no late night rendezvous with her. But she was a part of his other sick behavior. He'd make all of them come into the bathroom from time to time when he was bathing. He'd stretch out in the tub and fondle himself while all three girls stood just inches from its edge and watched. And they'd better watch. One down turned glance or blink that lasted too long and he'd reach out and yank them by their arms and back to attention.

At twenty three years of age, Carmen was a woman who was getting married with no understanding of how a woman was supposed to please a man, and sex was revolting for her. She knew how to cook, how to clean, how to mend holes in socks and keep the wash done. But as far as it concerned Carmen, she considered herself to still be a virgin and really had no desire to change that status.

And that is what she had told Herschel to keep him off of her while he courted her. Because he was a gentleman, he respected her wishes to be untouched until after they took their vows, and showed her how much he loved her in other ways; a jewel adorned bracelet here, a silk scarf or a half dozen roses there. And now that he had made Carmen his wife, she was expected to give him her newness, say yes to his desire to taste the sweetness she had withheld from him, always remaining steadfast through so many nights of no's.

She stood at the altar, barely hearing what the minister was saying, contemplating if she'd ever be able to tell Herschel the truth about her not-so-unbroken virginity, and worrying if he'd be able to feel that she had already been spoiled a dozen times. Would he confront her if he discovered her walls to be too easy to penetrate, proof that someone else had been there? The fear of what her first experience would be like with a man other than her father paralyzed her, and in all the times Herschel had told her of how he fantasized about her in his dreams, she never once found sexual urges for him lurking around inside of her. She prayed every night that she wasn't rigid, already dried up at her age.

She knew how much her new husband wanted to consummate their promise of forever after. She wanted to be able to will her body to connect to the fever she knew existed just under Herschel's surface, she wanted to be able to reciprocate the energy she felt radiating from him when he'd hold her close in a goodbye embrace at the end of a date, never once getting beyond the hug, a brief kiss or the front door of her apartment.

Carmen gained coherence just as the minister was saying, "By the powered vested in me by the state of Ohio, and as a man of God, I now pronounce you man and wife. Herschel Kellogg you may now kiss your bride." She could feel that familiar yearning rise up and out of Herschel as he pulled her into his fire right there in front of the entire congregation of Greater Good. Her lips puckered in obedience, just as she had vowed to be, but didn't really kiss him back.

The "I do's" were said, the bouquet tossed, the wedding cake simultaneously smashed into the new couples faces, and finally she and Herschel were ascending the escalator to the mezzanine level of The Cincinnatian Hotel, a monument of sorts that was erected smack dab in the center of the shopping district of downtown. The hotel had opened its doors in 1928 and had been there through the changing and renaming of businesses around it, the cement paving of the cobblestone street in front of it, and the Great Depression, and five decades later it was still standing and still the most beautifully designed and decadent structure in the city.

On the way to the room that would serve as their honeymoon layover suite, Carmen momentarily felt like she was going to regurgitate her wedding dinner stepping off the escalator onto plush, velvet-like carpet that made a slightly annoying, crunching sound each time a foot was lowered onto it. The courage to take each step came just as the steps were being made, not one second sooner, and she fought the heaving urge to tear her arm from Herschel's grasp and run to the down escalator, descending it in leaps and bounds like the clock was about to strike midnight and the fairytale would be over.

With plans for just an overnight stay before flying out the next morning for the Bahamas, their final honeymoon destination, everything Carmen needed for the evening was easily tucked into the small overnight case given to her by her three bridesmaids; her two sisters and her best friend, Janice. Inside that case were a change of panties for the next morning, a frilly little sundress and strappy flat sandals for the flight, her makeup bag, her toiletries, including the scented soap and body splash purchased especially for this night, and the champagne colored negligee that Janice had given to Carmen especially from her, for that very special first night with Herschel.

She had all the pieces in place, so Carmen had decided to give her best effort to the events that lay ahead, and somehow began to feel charged under the surge of thinking she might just succeed at pulling this off. Maybe she could fake it well enough to hide her fear until she learned how to ease into his longings for her and reciprocate like any normal woman should.

Herschel carried a hanging garment bag across the fold of his arm. A small bag that held his few grooming necessities swung from the fingers of the arm that held the bag, and he wore a smile so wide and telling that anyone who'd take the time to look at him would know that he was a man on a mission, his tunnel vision focused on getting out of the public and into his first private night with his beautiful and virtuous wife.

One night, just three weeks before the big day, Janice and Carmen sat sipping on some wine in the perfectly square living room of the apartment she would soon share with her husband. She'd summoned the nerve to ask Janice to show her how to move and what to say while her husband was making love to her.

Carmen knew that Janice knew men like she knew her own name, backward and forward and inside and out. Janise Dumont had a round behind that looked like it had been filled with an air pump. It bounced when she walked in unison with breast that sat snuggly in C size cups and arguably would fit better into a D cup. She was an average looking girl, but moved her curves expertly, like a woman aware of the magnetic power of the fat-lipped pussy laying squeezed between her thunderous thighs. She had all the right features to make a man do almost anything to get it, and they usually did and she usually gave it up. She wasn't a whore, not really. She was just in touch with her sexuality and unashamed of it like the society we lived in back then told us a woman like her should be.

Carmen had thought Janice would demonstrate by standing up and gyrating her own body while instructing Carmen to mimic her, but Janice had snatched Carmen off the sofa and grabbed her by the hips and pushed them back and thrust them forward, then moved the bottom portion of her body in a slow circular motion and told her to dip like she was hoolah hooping. Janice also told her to moan, and say Herschel's name a few times once he really started to get into his groove. And she reminded Carmen to open her mouth when she kissed him because a closed lipped kiss was for daddy, not for her husband. Carmen wanted to tell Janice that not all fathers keep their mouths closed and their tongues in their mouths when they kissed their daughters.

Dispelling those negative thoughts, even if only for this night, Carmen swallowed the last of her fear as she and Herschel entered the hotel room holding hands and crossing the threshold as Mr. and Mrs. Kellogg. But she had hardly dropped her bag to the floor when Herschel grabbed her around the waist and pulled her against his already erect manhood. When he had found the time to put down the items that he was holding, Carmen did not know and didn't have the time to figure out. His erection startled Carmen and she tried to push her butt out so that her pelvis was not in direct contact with his hard-on, but Herschel refused to let loose of this precious moment or his newly possessed wife. His urgency was in full visibility tonight, and Herschel would no longer wait. He readjusted his lock on her waist so that his forearms pushed right into her lower back and held her right up next to him, causing Carmen to feel the whole length of his penis.

The little bit of nerve that had somehow started to peek in the pit of her belly on the way to the room, dissipated in that instant. Her body stiffened and her eyes widened two times their normal size. If he had bothered to look in her face at that very moment instead of burying his face between her breasts, he'd have seen the fear there. Missing the opportunity to comprehend that the reaction he felt in his wife was not excitement like his erection convinced him it was, Herschel lifted Carmen in one swift motion and spun her around as he moved quickly towards the bed. His fingers worked to unzip her dress and he slid her arms free of its sleeves as he placed her back on her feet, allowing the dress to fall away from the top of her body and expose the lacey black bra underneath.

Herschel laid Carmen directly in the bed's center, and gazed at her hungrily. She had a mind to run now that she was out of his grasp, but the flames of fire she could literally see burning in his pupils halted her. She mistook the burning of the passion a man is supposed to have dancing in his eyes when glimpsing his new bride lying across their honeymoon bed for something sinister, much like the expression she'd imagined must have been in her own father's eyes before he'd mount her.

In surprisingly controlled movements that defied his yearning appetite, Herschel began to tug at the wedding dress Carmen had been confined in for the past 8 hours. The garment slid over her modestly full hips faster than it looked like it should have, and in a matter of seconds, Carmen lay on the bed partially exposed in black bikini panties made of silk, and the push up bra that also matched the panties in fabric. He paused just long enough to yank off his wedding suit piece by piece in what seemed like a race to be first to the finish line and did not stop until he was completely naked. Stroking the head of his dick, he crawled into the bed and starting at her feet, he kissed a path to her lips, pressing every inch of his body into hers as he slid up her frame.

As soon as they were face to face, he began devouring her mouth with his own, taking Carmen's very breath away. Using his tongue to explore the roof of her mouth, her gums and her tongue, the weight of his body and the grinding motion he had begun to do with his hips, pushed her thighs apart, and overwhelmed with the ferocious hunger of long endured anticipation, he pushed her panties to the side with his fingers and plunged inside of her tight and barely moist vagina, dried from rigidity and, in that moment, fear.

Carmen meant to tell Herschel that she needed a moment. She had been laying there trying to find her voice to ask him to slow down. It was all happening too quickly. She thought she'd at least get to change into her lingerie that had, after all, been personally selected and given to her especially for this night. But after just 10 minutes into the episode, the concern for the lingerie slipped from her mind. Just as Herschel had found his rhythm and began to move in time to the tempo of the blood coursing through the shaft of his rock solid penis, Carmen faded into a familiar trance and she could hear the same tune in her head that she'd hummed to herself as a little girl.

She forgot to pump, to wind and dip her hips, to reciprocate. In fact, she just laid there, still and detached, emotionless and numb, a familiar demeanor to her when it was her father on the giving end. Carmen never got around to panting

Herschel's name or moaning her approval of how he was making her feel. She only remembered to say those familiar words; the only words she had in her repertoire, those mindlessly muttered words that the only other man who had ever known her body in this way liked to hear. "Oh, Daddy Grey, Daddy Grey, Daddy Grey," the words spilled out so fluidly, Carmen didn't even realize she was saying them.

And as soon as Herschel heard the monotone, robotic way his new wife had just called out her father's name, his erection immediately softened. She saw him scramble off of her and off of the bed, right before Carmen was catapulted from her nightmare and back into the realm of the conscious.

****

Separated from her aunt by only a hallway linen closet and a bathroom, Merci lay restless and distressed in the full size bed with the over bleached sheets that emulated the heady fumes of spring scented Clorox. The smell of the blanket that her aunt had pulled out of the cedar chest at the foot of the bed contrasted the cleanliness of the sheets, and revealed how long it had been since someone had stayed overnight in her aunt's house.

Merci had not had a good night's sleep since she had gotten to Cincinnati and it was starting to take a toll on her. Irritability tugged at her nerves making her feel unbalanced. Periodically throughout that day, while cleaning the house, she had had to hold onto pieces of the furniture to steady herself, and feeling the dizziness at that moment, Merci was grateful to be laying down.

Her mind was as consumed as her body was weary, and her emotions were drained. But as much as she wanted to sleep, the last few dreams she'd had were enough to make her resist for just a little while longer. Besides, her thoughts were running rampant and they mostly revolved around what she would say in 12 hours to lay her mother's body to rest. Merci lay there with her eyes closed, thinking and praying to the God she did not believe in for a muse of some sort.

Merci spoke into the darkness of the bedroom and broke the resonating quiet that made her thoughts too easy to hear, "What did I really know about you Charlotta Samuel?" She paused, and as if expecting a response, she scanned the shadows of the furniture being cast on the walls from the streak of moonlight that shown meekly through the sheer curtain hanging at the only window in the room.

When no response materialized from the darkness, Merci rolled over and turned on the lamp sitting on the nightstand next to the bed. She propped herself up on the pillows and rubbed her eyes, trying to adjust them to the light. There was a notepad and a pen in her bag and she needed to write. Writing had always been her balance beam, her way to make as much sense out of her life as it was possible to make, or at least create a livable justification for what would never make sense. She fumbled her way out of the bed, shuffled through the outside pocket of her suitcase and seconds later with pen and pad in hand, she returned to the warmth of the bed and began scribbling phrases on an empty page.

At first, the words were just marks on the page, not really accumulating into a cohesive composition; just scattered descriptions of the kind of mother Merci wished Charlotta could have been. She understood the obstacle that loomed over Charlotta and prevented her from feeling true love for her one and only offspring, but understanding never diluted the hurt that ate away at Merci's insides.

Merci kept writing, oblivious to the danger zone she was entering, tumbling through the steep slope of her thoughts and dredging up images that she had long ago pushed deep down into her soul where they hid from the judgment of the world. Tears began to burn her eyes and slid like hot oil down her cheeks, dropping onto the note pad in her lap, smearing the ink and blurring her sight. She gripped the pen laced between her fingers so tightly that her hand began to get numb. Still, she continued until the broken phrases began to resemble order.

When the final word had been written, what lie in front of Merci was not a eulogy but a letter to Charlotta. She read over it, as it was her nature to do. Being an editor for the last ten years of her professional career had instilled an expectation of perfect grammar and punctuation in even her own written endeavors, and she knew she would not sleep until each and every sentence had been perused and corrected, despite the fact that the person to whom the letter was addressed would never read it. She read the letter aloud.

Dear Charlotta,

The sanity I've fought to maintain is on the verge of crashing down around me, and just like always, you're not here to help me through it. I thought your death would bring me some closure, some relief from the stress of carrying our dysfunction around with me for so long. But it is too encompassing and no matter how hard I try to force it into extinction, it resurfaces time and time again, leaving me with a calloused soul and detached from any form of pure human connection. A girl-child is supposed to learn how to love from her mother and learn how to be loved from her father. Any hope I ever had of grasping those concepts through experience was thwarted long ago by the discovery of who I am, who my father was, and who you decided to be. I know you were a victim too, and maybe retreating into nothingness was your way of escaping the torment of your reality. But I needed you; needed you like living things need oxygen to breathe, and you never found a way to give me what I needed. Grey Samuel was sick, but you were diseased with a festering numbness that prevented you from ever seeing me as more than a result of his illness.

Why didn't I matter to you? Why couldn't you see how much

I longed to be close to you? Why didn't you take me with you when you left? Why didn't you send for me when you returned? How could you just abandon me, leaving me to figure it all out on my own? I ask these questions as I have asked them a million times before, knowing that there is no explanation or response you could offer that would make the hurt disappear, no salve that would soothe the scars etched into my psyche, as permanent as the six feet of earth that will separate us forever. Maybe if I stop asking, the need to know will go away. And maybe if I stop remembering, I'll go to my own grave pretending like I am free. It sure seems to have worked for you. But I'm not free and your death doesn't let you off the hook either. There is no solace to be gained from your departure from the living. Your death will carry the stain of the hurt you left behind and you will never rest in peace as long as this chaos exists in me. I'll see you in hell.

Merci

Merci folded the paper in half and placed it on the nightstand, not sure of what she expected it to prove or what she would do with it. But she somehow felt vindicated and, at last, able to sleep. And even though she still had not decided on what to say to eulogize her mother, she turned off the lamp and drifted off into the first dreamless sleep she had had in two days.

****

Miles across town, Camille lay in her bed with the covers over her head trying not to peek from under them for the one hundredth time to check the time on the cable box. The tick of the wall clock she had hanging in the master bathroom that was attached to her bedroom seemed loud and intrusive in the resounding silence of the condo and she lay there inhaling the fresh coat of paint she had given the walls just three days before, hoping it would alter her mind state towards a highness that would put her into a stupor powerful enough to make her sleep through tomorrow. She feared the Valiums she had on reserve would not be enough.

Dealing with her family had always made Camille shake inside with an anger she didn't understand. She wanted to understand why her nerves trembled so violently whenever she had to be around, think about or otherwise be involved in any kind of way with the only other people on this entire earth that she could call blood relatives. But she was always so easily undone by the convulsive tremors in her belly that making sense of it was hard to do. Her anger lived with her, it moved with her. When she turned, it turned. When she ran, it ran. It was ever-present and had a stronghold on her that tightened around her throat like a noose and often made it difficult for her to breathe. And sometimes it literally made her physically ill to the point that she'd hurl, or gag on her saliva when there was no food in her stomach to regurgitate. So the Valium helped and they were prescribed so she was both legal and happy.

She was not like Carmen or Charlotta. Both had

found a way to push their anger and hurt out, and had learned to live what appeared to the world to be happy, or at least somewhat adjusted lives. Camille's anger ran deep. It had grown roots and planted itself inside of her. And she had long ago accepted it as a way of life. It was as natural to her as breathing and sometimes seemed equally as essential to her life.

Camille had thought that changing her last name would render her some relief, but it hadn't. She had thought that moving out to the far east suburb of Eastgate would help her escape the festering anger, but the hole that had been bore in her center hadn't healed. She had thought that having sex with women would calm the sense of madness that pulled at her spirit, but that had only made her gay. So she gave up trying and held on tight to the only feeling she had ever known like it was her only lifeline. Anger had become her very heartbeat and now she couldn't imagine living without it. Camille wished that she could have been smart enough to leave Cincinnati like Charlotta and her niece Merci had found the strength to do. But in her heart she knew that there was no place far enough away that she could go where the anger wouldn't follow and find her.

Camille lay there turning from one side to the other, wrestling with her decisions and wondering how she ever thought any of them was going to cure the incurable. Replaying the episodes that led to her destructive path made her remember the first time she realized that she was harboring not only anger but also jealousy, and that jealousy made her even angrier. The cycle was never-ending and thinking about it now kept Camille awake and curled up under her covers in a nauseating heap of nervous tension for another whole hour until she finally got up out of bed and dry swallowed two of her happy pills.

Like Jorja Sweet, Charlotta, Carmen and Merci, Camille had also experienced a solitary moment of realization, of understanding how the family's havoc had permanently scarred her. Her defeating discovery happened when she was 27-years-old. Camille was leaving her job as a medical assistant at the Planned Parenthood Clinic feeling the fatigue of the day and desperately wanting to get home to a beer, her bed and re-runs of Good Times, The Jeffersons, and Sanford and Son.

As she stood on the sidewalk waiting to pass through the picket line of pro-life protestors who gathered there every day trying to lure the young women away from their decision to abort the mistakes they had made, she was approached by a woman with a card in her hand. The woman asked Camille to give her card to the doctors in the clinic and was saying something about offering her services, free of charge. According to her business card, the woman was a therapist who worked with a private network of professionals who specialized in rehabilitation for abused women. She was a head doctor skilled specifically and in general for women who were at a crossroad in their lives for one reason or another. Camille had taken the business card of the pink-faced, pencil-thin therapist without saying thank you and pushed passed her in a mad dash to her car.

One day, about a month later, Camille was sitting in her living room making steady progress through a 12-bottle case of Budweiser and retreating into unconsciousness from the mixture of the alcohol and the Valiums she had swallowed. She sat there numbly engaged by thoughts of the five one-night stands she'd had over the last few weeks with women she had picked up at a local lesbian bar. She couldn't remember what they looked like and their names escaped her too. Camille felt tired from the thoughts that crawled slowly through her mind but wasn't sure if it was the constant cocktail of booze and pills or her overactive, dysfunctional sex life that was causing the feeling.

Just as the drugs and alcohol had begun to take their full affect, a commercial about depression came on the TV and in a momentary flash of blurred semi-alertness she remembered the card she had gotten from that therapist at the clinic. Camille sure felt depressed. It wasn't as if she didn't know that she was alcohol and drug dependent, though functional. She knew she should be disgusted with the disregard with which she treated women, but nothing inside of her could manage to care. Maybe she needed the help of a therapist more than the young women who came in and out of the clinic in droves. She decided to give the objective ear of a trained specialist a try.

Three days later, Camille was walking into the therapist's office on legs that had turned into jelly the moment she stepped out of her car. The oatmeal she had eaten that morning was sitting in a ball in the pit of her stomach refusing to begin the digestive process. She was sweating but felt clammy and cold despite the warm spring sun that was beating down on her head and back. She blindly pushed on the door to the doctor's office and floated to the front desk. She could barely hear herself tell the receptionist her name or that she was there to see Dr. Patel because the pulse in her ears was thumping loudly in a relentless rhythm opposite the uneven pounding of her heart. She could not believe she had come here to tell some stranger about the disgusting truth that was her family. But before she could change her mind and run from the office to escape the panic of her decision, the receptionist was calling her name and telling her that the doctor would see her now.

As Camille entered the room her attention was drawn to her left at the sound of the doctor's voice welcoming her by name and an offer for Camille to join her on the side of the office she was occupying. Dr. Patel was standing in front of a deep burgundy leather chair in a simple blue leisure pants suit. She seemed thinner to Camille than she did when she'd seen her for the first time at the clinic. Camille's warped sense of humor immediately made her consider if she'd have sex with the doctor, but as she moved closer and could see the doctor better, she decided that the answer to her question was no. Camille preferred women with color in their skin and some kind of curves. Dr. Patel had neither. In fact, she seemed to glow next to the heavy color of the chair. Camille moved in the doctor's direction and shook her extended hand with a smile anyway and politely introduced herself.

Dr. Patel's office looked exactly like the typical shrink's office; dark furniture and dim lighting. On one side of the room was a reasonable sized desk behind which sat floor to ceiling cherry oak bookcases that were filled with books about mental states and self-healing techniques. In front of the desk were a couple of straight back chairs where the therapist probably held meetings with her staff, or with the family members of clients when diagnosis and treatments were being discussed. On the other side of the office was the patient therapy area that housed the leather seat for the doctor, a matching sofa for the patient positioned directly across from the chair, a coffee table between the two, and a squared-shaped side table next to the doctor's chair. There was a small desk lamp that illuminated that area of the office, and the separate sides of the room were split right in the middle by a lone window. The shades at the window were slightly opened, letting in just enough natural sunlight from outside to light the rest of the office.

Despite the sparse furnishings, the room was warm and oddly cozy. The ambiance helped Camille to relax a little. Dr. Patel took her seat as Camille made her way to the sofa. She stood there for a few seconds trying to figure out how she was supposed to stretch out on a sofa with arms on both sides. Camille thought there'd be a chaise lounge. Isn't that the usual in a shrink's office? She contemplated a few seconds longer then looked back at Dr. Patel. The doctor did not say anything, she only shoved her hands in Camille's direction indicating that she could go ahead and get comfortable. So she did. Camille assumed the position she believed she was supposed to. Despite that Camille was tall for a woman, comparable in height to her father, she squeezed her body onto the sofa the best she could and prepared herself to be emotionally plucked and prodded for the next hour.

Camille allowed her left arm to hang off the sofa's edge instead of resting it across her belly, her head lay on one arm of the sofa and she bent her knees over the other end so that her feet dangled awkwardly. Camille lay there, turned slightly away from the chair that Dr. Patel sat in just feet from her with crossed legs and pen and pad in hand. Camille's other arm lay squeezed between her body and the back of the sofa, but despite her seemingly uncomfortable positioning, she felt rested.

Dr. Patel cleared her throat and giggled a little once

Camille was settled down, knowing that Camille was behaving based on some movie perception of what patients do in her situation. The laugh made Camille turn to look at the doctor with an inquisitive expression of confusion on her face.

"I don't mean to giggle, please forgive me Ms. Patterson. But I haven't ever had a patient attempt to lie down on that sofa. You don't have to lie down. That's really a myth about therapists' offices. There isn't typically a chaise and patients don't typically lay down."

Camille wouldn't normally stand for being laughed at or mocked, but she decided not to ask the doctor if she thought that shit was funny or if she considered herself to be some kind of comedian. Camille simply sat up, smoothed her pants out, crossed her legs with her ankle resting on her knee and apologized, but counted Dr. Patel's laughter at her as the first strike against the doctor.

The room was quiet for what seemed like a long time; so quiet that Camille tuned into the chirping of the birds fluttering around outside the window in the bushes of purple and pink spring flowers. Camille sat on the sofa with her eyes staring into her lap, wondering if she was supposed to speak first. Just as she cleared her throat to say something, although she had no idea what that something was going to be, Dr. Patel began speaking in a hushed but audible tone.

"Welcome, Ms. Patterson." Dr. Patel drew out the *s* in Ms. with an extended *z* sound and Camille immediately felt agitated by the doctor's voice. But she did not shift her head to look at Dr. Patel, preferring instead not to look her in the eye; she wasn't sure what the doctor would see in them.

Dr. Patel continued, "I have to admit, I didn't expect that the next time I'd see you would be in a patient capacity and I'm interested to find out what brought you here. But if you need me to help you with something, then I am really glad you came in to see me today."

Camille breathed a heavy sigh but remained quiet and still. She didn't like being referred to as a patient. That implied that she was sick and that was something she was not willing to acknowledge. Was she supposed to say thank you for the offer of her help? *Did* she really have something that she needed help with? Sitting there getting ready to tell this woman all of her business, Camille was no longer sure

Dr. Patel interrupted her quiet again as if she was totally oblivious to the fact that Camille had not yet uttered a word, "Why don't we start by you telling me why you decided to seek therapy."

Camille's agitation grew, but she managed to mouth a response. "If I knew why I was here, would I need to be here? Didn't your card say you specialized in women who have been abused or something? Then wouldn't that suggest to you that I must be abused in some way. I will tell you this right now. If I have to diagnose myself I am not paying your ass."

Dr. Patel was not fazed by Camille's outburst as she was used to patients being on edge and testy with her. She simply responded, "You have a point Mzzzz Paterson." The doctor chuckled and wrote something down on her pad. She started over.

"So let me start again with a more deliberate question. Why did you keep my card instead of giving it to the doctors like I asked you to? You obviously are not pregnant, confused, and contemplating abortion. Yet, you still felt compelled to consider therapy. But like you said, you must be abused. Confused maybe? Or maybe you feel suicidal. No, I think more like homicidal. Awww, on second thought you must be consumed by a sexual appetite that you can't seem to control, or better yet, sexually repressed. Yes, that is it! Sexual dysfunction, right?"

Dr. Patel was trying a little sarcasm of her own and it pissed Camille off. A normally functioning mind that did not thrive on anger may have been able to share a little chuckle with the doctor, but Camille reverted to the emotion that she knew best and most.
She snorted, "Sexually repressed! That's funny."
Camille was staring right at the doctor's face now.

"I'm not sexually repressed. That's my sister Carmen. I get plenty of sex! So take that out of your head. Now, I don't think sex is some kind of spiritual experience intended to transfix the souls of men like my sister Charlotta did. But I digress. To answer your inquiry about why I used your card, I used your card because I'm always angry and I'm tired of feeling this way."

"Hmmm ok," Dr. Patel wrote something else down on her pad. "So…"

"Wait, I'm not done," Camille interrupted the doctor's attempt at responding. "You want to know so much and I'm paying you to listen, so listen. I'm gay and I have random sex with women I barely know or don't know at all, then kick them out of my house before the remnants from their orgasms can dry up. I am the daughter of a deviant father and a mother who stayed with him despite his sickness. He was a mean son of a bitch who beat my mother, and she never did one damn thing to change her situation. Oh yeah, and he was a pedophile who had sex with his daughters, both of them, Charlotta and Carmen. Then he impregnated my sister, Charlotta. Charlotta died a week ago, and she should be happy that she's finally free of this world and its ugliness."

Never pausing and barely inhaling between sentences, Camille continued, "Her daughter…his daughter, Merci, came to town two days ago after 15 years of being away, and she looks just like my perverted father and my flower child sister. The resemblance is weird not just because it's unnatural but because she's beautiful in spite of the pure repulsiveness she was made from."

Camille felt like she wanted to cry, but she was not the kind of woman who was comfortable with her feelings or in touch enough with them to even realize that the burning in her sinuses was tears needing to be shed. She breathed in heavily and for the first time, and rubbed at her nose as if she was trying to stifle a sneeze. When Camille spoke again it was with a cracking voice.

"My father never had intercourse with me. I guess I was the saved one. He fondled me and talked nasty to me and made me come in the bathroom with him when he bathed like he'd done to both of my sisters, but then Charlotta got pregnant. I was too young for him to have begun having intercourse with. His rule was to wait until we were 12 years old to start actually penetrating us, and I was three months from eleven when she got pregnant, after which he was miraculously unable to get it up anymore. I must have been the saved one, right?"

Camille paused. She was beginning to feel that oppressive tired again. She knew she couldn't fit on the sofa but she suddenly felt like she wanted to lie back down. Dr. Patel was writing and indicating she either heard or understood with the occasional *hmmm*. When the doctor spoke again, Camille was finally ready to listen.

"Camille, sometimes our past consumes our present. At some point we all have to decide not to let our past define how we live in the here and now, but we've got to want to be free. I think you love your family but you aren't sure if they love you. Have you ever talked to them or ask them how they feel about you? Have you ever told them how you feel about the abuse or about the way they have chosen to deal with their own pain? You may come to understand things about your sisters that you perceived differently."

It sounded like good advice, but Camille was only half listening. She had taken enough of a breath and was ready to talk again. She had lived silently behind her clown's antics for far too long so to have someone finally listening opened a Pandora's Box in her soul that didn't want to be closed up right then.

"You know, everyone found a way to turn their madness into some suitable living space. And the little lost child, not really special for any reason, is…" Camille searched for the words. "Well, hell, she's trying to squeeze herself on a sofa that is too small for her to fit on."

Dr. Patel offered a different viewpoint. "It sounds like, to me, everyone closed the chapters in their lives that they didn't write, and they escaped. And the truth is that while they seem to be living comfortably, you won't know if they have or if they can help you do the same if you do not talk to them."

Camille was so emotionally exhausted that she laid her head back on the sofa but continued. "My sister Charlotta just checked the hell out permanently, even before she died. I mean, she walked out of the life she was born into and never looked back to see if anyone else had been left there. My sister Carmen walks around pretending like our family is not fucked up. Her cover-up is bullshit because I know she hates him like I do. Merci left Cincinnati and we haven't seen her since. She's back to bury her mother, but she buried the hatchet a long time ago. And I'm just angry all the time; all day, every single God damn day of my miserable life!"

By the time Camille had gotten it all out, her chest was heaving with exasperation. Her head lay on the back on the sofa and she was staring at the ceiling but not really seeing it. She finally lowered her head to look at Dr. Patel. The doctor sat there, calm and composed, completely unaffected by the things she had heard. Camille guessed that the doctor had probably heard worse in her professional lifetime, but couldn't imagine what worse could possibly be.

"Well," Dr. Patel began again, "Your anger is understandable, and the basic root of your anger is obvious. Your father spread more than his seed through your family. His behavior was despicable and because he was never really held accountable, it's been hard for your family to deal with it. But the question is what are you most angry about?"

"I'm angry about it all! What kind of dumb ass question is that anyway? Shouldn't I be angry about it all? You say it's understandable? No shit doc!"

"Yes, Mzzzz Patterson, you have every right to be angry about it all. But you said yourself that you had been saved. Your father never got the chance to have sex with you. It seems you'd find some comfort in that."

"Comfort!" Camille's tone was still elevated and her throat was beginning to hurt from the octave she was using. "I'm beginning to doubt your skills doc. How could I find comfort in the middle of all that deviance?"

"I know your father hurt you and pedophilia is a sickness that deteriorates and shreds normalcy. But he never had sex with you Camille."

Camille was happy that she hadn't called her Mzzzz Patterson again, but she was getting sick of talking about who her father had sex with and who he had not.

Dr. Patel continued, "That doesn't diminish the affects of what he did do to you or of what he did to your sisters and your mother. But I'll say it again and this time I want you to tell me how it makes you feel. He never had sex with you Camille."

"Well, why not?" Camille started ranting but she couldn't really hear herself. The volcano that had laid dormant in the pit of her body had finally exploded and she was about to spew the saddest truth she'd ever spoke all over Dr. Patel.

"Why didn't he want to have sex with me? Is that supposed to make me feel special or something? Whoop-dee-fucking-do for me! After Charlotta laid up and got herself pregnant, it was all everybody could talk about. What were we going to do about the baby? What were the people in the neighborhood going to say about the baby? Would our sick little secret be revealed? And Carmen became mama's favorite because she joined mama in her crusade to save face like that was really possible. And Daddy Grey, well he just started ignoring us all. So what was missing from the equation doc? I'll tell you what was missing! Me! They forgot about me. Ever been lonely in a house full of people doc? Huh? Have you? And you have the nerve to suggest that the fact that he didn't want to have sex with me should comfort me. What the fuck is that doc?"

"In fact, I believe it should." Dr. Patel was so matter-of-fact in her response that Camille just sat there staring at her with wide eyes and a hanging bottom lip. "But it's not what I think that counts. At first you said that he *couldn't* have sex with you due to impotency. Then you asked me why he did not *want* to have sex with you. If not relieved, how does that make you feel?"

Camille had had it with this Dr. Patel and exploring her feelings. She glared hard at the therapist hoping that the heat from her stare would penetrate right through her skin and turn her chalky complexion liquid.

"Are you suggesting that I wanted him to have sex with me?" Camille was appalled.

"I'm not suggesting anything Camille. I'm repeating what you said back to you so that you can hear it and process how you really feel about it." Dr. Patel jotted a few more notes then put her pen and pad down on the side table. "Our hour has come to an end, but I'm giving you some homework for our next session. I want you to start keeping a journal and write in it every day. For each entry, I want you to start out by writing one sentence about something you remember from your childhood. Then write how the incident or sentiment made you feel then, and how it makes you feel now. Be as detailed as you can. My job is to make sure I get you ready to share it with your sisters so they can share with you how they feel about the same things. Often times, people see things differently, so they handle them differently."

Camille sat up, dropped her crossed leg, put her elbows on her knees and looked directly in the doctor's eyes. "There won't be another session so take your homework assignment and shove it up your ass. Since you're so big on feeling, see how *that* makes *you* feel!" Camille stormed out of the doctor's office in such a rage that she never even heard the receptionist yelling at her to stop so that she could set a date for her next appointment.

Camille got in her car and drove straight to the local lesbian bar. It was only one o'clock in the afternoon, but she needed a drink. She didn't expect to find anyone else there when she pushed through the doors, but as soon as she sat at the bar she noticed a woman sitting at the other end frowning at her. She ordered a Bloody Mary, deciding that it could serve as lunch since it was made with tomato juice, and drank it down so quickly the vodka burned in her chest. Just as she was getting ready to order another round, the woman at the other end of the bar sauntered over and took the stool next to Camille.

"So why haven't you called me?" The woman sounded indignant.

She obviously knew Camille but nothing about her seemed familiar. Camille spit her order at the bartender and rubbed her temples before asking the woman who the hell she was.

"I'm Patricia. We fucked five days ago. Are you telling me you don't remember tasting my cookie?"

Camille looked the woman up and down and her memory slowly came into focus. "Yeah, I guess I remember who you are. But I'm not in the mood to socialize right now."

The woman was stunned but slid off the stool and stood up to leave anyway. Before she walked out the door she turned back and told Camille not to bother calling her. Camille was glad to be let off the hook and drank down her second Bloody Mary as quickly as she had devoured the first.

As Camille drove the few blocks to her house feeling a little fuzzy from the drinks, tears began to roll down her face in uncontrollable streams. In between her sobs, she heard herself say, "Why didn't he want to have sex with me? He gave Charlotta and Carmen his special time, even gave Charlotta a baby. He didn't give me nothing! He didn't give me nothing but this stupid anger! Everybody got attention but me. They forgot about me!"

She hit the mailbox pulling into the driveway but didn't care. She ran in the house, slammed the door, still crying and with snot running out her nose and into her mouth. She didn't care about that either. She locked her door and didn't step a foot outside again for another two weeks. By the time she returned to the world of the living, she had lost her job and the last pieces of sanity she had.

****

Charlotta's body lay in the cold, enclosed casket she would be spending her eternity in as her spirit floated free of its inflexible confines and hovered overhead looking down at its own corpse. She sneered at the cheapness of the sateen fabric lining the coffin. She turned her nose up at the homely looking dress her sisters had laid her out in. It was nothing like what she would have worn to such an important occasion; her final farewell. The dress was concealing and stark white and she laughed at the irony of purity it cast.

Charlotta's attire was usually full of deep and vibrant colors that gave her body a sense of warmth and sensuality. She had a heightened awareness of her aura and was as free in her body as she was in her mind. But nothing about the clothes her dead body was wearing said anything about who she was. The pearls on her neck and in her ears were glass and there was an angel broach stuck on the dress that sparkled with far too many clear rhinestones. But worse of all, they were getting ready to bury her in a wig! A wig, of all things! Why couldn't they have let her natural and crowning glory be? Hadn't she suffered too much in her life for her ashes to have to rest in such gaudy, costume bullshit? Her spirit was aggravated and she wished she could lift her body from its death prison and give herself a makeover.

Her sisters knew nothing about her, not in life and not in death. There had always been a distance between them, stretched out and spread wide, rippling and ebbing like the ocean and making the love they should have had for one another a fading and watery thing taking on the form of the pain that existed between them. As her ghost hovered above her cold and cotton stuffed body, Charlotta was at least happy to be escaping that ever-present sadness that plagued her sisters and that they always seemed to be trying to burden her with too.

Didn't they understand that her locks were a part of her? They had been a part of her healing process, they chronicled every step she made and every level of liberation she had acquired. Something is seriously wrong with women who have no sense of who they are. Charlotta *knew* who she was, and she was quick to tell anyone who asked. She was the eldest daughter of Grey and Jorja Sweet Samuel. She was the bearer of her father's baby. She was the slightly apathetic mother whose indifference towards life created a lonely, withdrawn and afraid little girl who grew up to be a lonely, withdrawn and afraid young woman. She was a massage therapist, learned in the principles of pleasure and healing. She was the fully uninhibited sister, the constant student of life who chose not to be limited by her past of sexual dysfunction. She was the only one of anyone else in her family who was anchored by the acceptance of what is.

Her waist-length dreadlocks, dyed many colors over the years until finally being colored a honey brown hue before she died, were her pride and joy. Charlotta's fine textured hair had been the thorn in her side since she had taken over the upkeep of her own grooming at the age of 17. Though it was coal black, slightly wavier than the average Black girl, and often referred to by girls with thicker, tighter curls as "good hair", it had always given Charlotta hell. Too limp for pin-curled ringlets or to withstand the humidity and the wind, its soft curls too wardly to be styled in the carefully molded up-do's of the times. Instead of trying to fool with it Charlotta mostly wore her hair pulled back in a tight bun with an array of decorated hair pins and barrettes.

Her accelerated aggravation subsided as Charlotta allowed her memories to drift back to the first time she'd decided to escape her diseased past in search of a healing. She was 32 years old when she had gotten to Jamaica, and settled in the mountains of Mayfield, a community of weed growing and smoking, goat herding, river bathing, fish eating, lovemaking, peace-living Rhastafarians about an hour northeast of Negril. Upon her arrival, she saw the dreadlocked sisters and brothers living and breeding there, and instantly her hair problems were over. She started twisting her locks the very first night she got there. Sitting on a pallet temporarily serving as a mattress on the bedroom floor in the two roomed, wooden house that she was renting from the man who owned and operated Mayfield Falls, the tourist reservation up the west side of the mountain, she separated her hair into thick sections and double strand twisted each one.

Her landlord's name was Franklin and he had given her the blankets she used to make her floor bed. They smelled like frankincense, shea butter and weed, but she didn't care. She was in Jamaica, the beautifully and elusively erotic, easy going Caribbean. Her family and their persistently heavy load were thousands of miles away and she was tucked away in this secluded, rural countryside, getting ready to find only God knew what but sure it wouldn't be as stifling as the existence she had had up until then.

The pleasantly warm night, the chirping of the crickets in the brush under the single window in the front room of the house, the far off sound of the river running down the slopes and into the crevices of the deeply carved out mountains all added to the giddiness that had taken over her nerves the moment the plane had touched down in Montego Bay.

Charlotta, finally finished with her physical transformation, walked over to retrieve a bowl of stew from a short, narrow counter in the front room of the two room house that served as an efficiency-sized kitchenette area. The counter, situated in the right corner of the room farthest from the front door, held the double burner hot plate on which her meal sat simmering. The stew had been given to her by Franklin. He had called it brown meat stew and he had brought it over soon after she'd first arrived in his parish and took residence in the house. She found a spoon in the single drawer under the counter and returned to her pallet on the floor in the back room to partake.

Three spoonfuls in and she was interrupted by a knock on the door. Carefully placing the bowl on the floor next to the pile of blankets, Charlotta pulled herself up and padded barefoot across the clay floor to the front door. She swung the door open without even asking who it was. It seems the nature of peace around her had lulled Charlotta into a sense of safety. She could not imagine any sort of crime taking place in this oasis.

Franklin stood in the doorway looking down at her from his towering 6 foot vantage point above her. Charlotta felt instantly naked in the short, thin house dress she wore. The breeze from the outside whipped at her thighs and swirled the bottom of the dress around them. Franklin's eyes moved down her frame as if drawn to do so and noticeably raised his eyebrows as the thickness of her thighs came into his view. He managed to pull his eyes away and raked them across her body as he raised his head to meet her blushing face. The thickness of his patois coated her face as it spilled from between his lips.

"Irie. Mi no mean to bring boderation, mi come here fi see wha gwaan girl? Yuh cris?" Charlotta didn't understand his patois but he had a smile as intoxicating as any elixir she'd ever swallowed and it spread across his face like sunshine. Charlotta's nipples hardened under the thin layer of dress. She prayed that Franklin did not detect her instant stimulation.

Her voice betrayed her effort to be aloof, exposing how she'd been moved. "Thank you for the stew. It's very good. I was just having dinner now. Would you like to come in?" She moved to the side and made a gesture for him to enter, unsure of whether he was having as hard of time understanding her as she was him.

Charlotta couldn't believe she'd just invited a strange man into her home so quickly. But something about his demeanor assured her that he would be worthwhile company. She felt strangely comfortable in his presence and it stunned her to be so content around a man.

"Mi see you gwaan culture you up girl." He reached for her locks as she led him to the back room. This hard bodied, smooth skinned, midnight black man squatted on the pile of blankets twirling his fingers through her wavy strands, twisting the coils that would eventually become her locks, overflowing the energy around her and making her skin tingle fiercely. By the time he had finished playing in her hair, Charlotta purposely and willingly surrendered to the lure of the atmosphere and to the pull of the prickling just below her surface, hoping that it would be worth succumbing to.

Charlotta could tell that Franklin was feeling the energy too and before she could get the feeling in check, she found herself rolling around on the blankets. They had sticky, sweaty, lusty, imploding sex all night, off and on between dozing in and out of sleep. He rose at 5am to go and take care of some business at The Falls and later that day Franklin strolled by (because strolling is how these Jamaicans make their way along) with some of the best marijuana she had ever inhaled, rolled in a spiraled funnel of paper that he called a spliff, and a proposition. They smoked, made love again and then talked about the job he had come to offer her.

He had explained, through drags on another spliff and planting kisses on her neck and shoulders that one of the attractions at The Falls was what he referred to as a river walk. Tourist paid $20 per person to take a one-hour hike through the river that had maturally cut through the mountain and he wanted her to be a masseuse on the tour. She would sit along the banks of the river at the very end of the tour under a grass and bamboo hut with reggae music playing and fruit juice on chill waiting to give oil massages to the hikers as they exited the water.

Franklin had said that it was a perfect addition to the river tour and that Charlotta had the perfect hands for the job, then he proceeded to take her right hand and put it on his hardening penis. She stroked it while she looked up into his eyes and accepted the position, knowing that the only training she had had in the art of massage was the childhood duty she had been forced to do for her father when he came home from the bar drunk and horny.

Franklin had two wives, both of whom he failed to mention during their trysts on Charlotta's floor and whom she met when she accompanied him back to the reservation that afternoon, but again, she didn't care. The community was a self-sufficient village of people who shared their resources and their lives communally. Charlotta fell right into step with the polygamous community there without realizing that it wasn't a far stretch from the way she had grown up. What happened in the family, stayed in the family and everybody was expected to play their respective part.

The laws of polygamy denote that each woman had her own residence, but performed their wifely duties assigned according to seniority and rank. A woman named Harriett was the first of the wives Franklin had taken into his fold. She was the queen mother who had graduated from housewife and caretaker of the children to the family manager when he took his second wife Lila. Harriett was responsible for making sure that the other wives to come executed their respective roles. Harriett had married Franklin when they were both 24 years old. She had supported him through tried and failed attempts at several business endeavors until Jamaica's economy took a turn for the better and became a sought after vacation destination in the 70's. She had given

Franklin three boys and now in her late 40's, she was too old to bear anymore children and had earned the right to be the queen, laying back delegating and giving sage advice to the children and the younger mothers when needed.

Lila, the second of Franklin's wives, had taken over the role Harriett had previously occupied. She cooked, she cleaned, and she nurtured, fed, and assigned the daily chores to the children. Lila had given him a girl and was pregnant with a son when Charlotta had arrived and married into their family. Lila, although second in Franklin's 4-wife limit according to the rules of polygamy, was his youngest wife. She was 22 years old and full of that youthful energy that allowed her to be 7 months pregnant but still be able to run after children and remain diligent in her duties, smiling and humming tunes of contentment all the while.

Charlotta, being Franklin's third wife and barely in her 30's, was responsible for keeping him satisfied in the bedroom and working at the mountain attraction. He had sex with all of his wives, but Lila was young and not very experienced. She had stamina, but no finesse. Harriett was older and experienced but at the age where she was over the whole sex thing. Sex with her was infrequent and quick. But Charlotta was in her prime. She was old enough to know how to move because she learned to appreciate the woman-ness of her body and at the age when she wanted it often. She had command over her motion and was giving the kind of sex that women in their 30's are privy to – unselfish but also self satisfying. Franklin loved having sex with her the most and for him she was one step closer to total fulfillment in a life fit for a providing man who was chief of his tribe.

Charlotta would have had to split the housework and childrearing with Lila if she wasn't being employed at The Falls. Lila didn't have any employable skills, but she was a teacher by instinct. She performed her other chores out of duty, but truly enjoyed the time she spent with the children giving the boys their reading lessons and teaching the girls how to become wives. Charlotta wouldn't be required to have more than one child since it would be a long time before Lila would no longer safely be able to. One child was her moral responsibility and unspoken expected contribution to the family. This new life was reflecting Charlotta's real family more than she was able to see.

When the time had come for Charlotta to give her family a child, however, 4 years into her living arrangement, it was discovered that Charlotta couldn't get pregnant. The village mid-wife had confirmed that her uterus was titled, and her womb was barren after an examination to figure out what was wrong. Charlotta was secretly happy to find out that she couldn't have any more children, although she couldn't explain to Franklin how her organs had come to be twisted and broken.

Franklin had never inquired before then and when she feigned unknowing, he didn't push. She never told him that she already had a child and that during the labor she had suffered some complications that moved her uterus out of place. Charlotta told him nothing about what her life was like before she had climbed that mountainside and just walked onto his tourist reservation, not looking like she had been sightseeing at all and seeming to have appeared out of thin air like a mirage.

The first time Franklin had seen her, he was taken in immediately by the glow surrounding her aura. Being the self-proclaimed tribal spiritualist that he was – living off the land, smoking the natural leaves of the Cannabis tree, and exploiting the erotic exoticism of the island by offering what he called the healing treatment as a tourist attraction – Franklin could see the special dripping off of Charlotta who was leaning against a bamboo tree at a low rising part of the river trying to catch her breath and looking radiant from the way the sun picked up the glisten of the sweat on her bare shoulders exposed by the halter-topped sun dress she wore.

Charlotta slid down into the water and emerged herself in its waist deep level. She let the skirt of her dress float on its surface, allowing the gentle motion to push the fabric towards her torso and away from her thighs. She cupped water into her cottony, fluffy hair, making it more wavy than it already was, and let the droplets run down her face and neck to her breasts that were free of a bra under the thin dress and bobbing on the water's softly flowing current.

Franklin wanted her immediately and willed his legs to move towards her. He leaned on the tree she had previously used as a crutch and commented on how pretty her shoulders were, transfixed by the nut color of her skin and the conflicted wavy hair that she now brushed her hands through, disheveling it and puffing it out even more. The schoolgirl smile Charlotta had flashed after the compliment sealed it for him. Franklin talked to Charlotta long enough to find out that she had purchased a one way ticket from the United States and had come to Jamaica with no particular plan. He figured out the rest; whatever Charlotta was leaving behind in America must not have been much to stay for but he'd make sure her choice to settle on this island was worth whatever journey she had taken to get here.

A few minutes more of conversation revealed that Charlotta was in search of a place to live while she figured out what was next. She had left the small, native-owned resort that she had stayed in the night before down in the cliffs above Negril early that morning and had been walking around ever since from parish to parish looking for one that suited her spirit. She had been told about a little community up the mountain by the cab driver who had brought her from the airport in Montego Bay to Negril. After having walked around for what seemed like hours,

Charlotta was grateful that she had kept the cabbies number. She'd called him as soon as she had gotten back to the hotel room she had rented and he was there within minutes to take her into the mountain.

Franklin told Charlotta to feel free to look around Mayfield and if it pleased her, he knew of a place she might be interested in. Charlotta looked at his warm smile and strong shoulders exposed by his shirtless torso and turning a new hue of charcoal under the sun, and took him up on his offer, choosing her living quarters (and eventually her living arrangement) sight unseen.

Franklin offered Charlotta a small dwelling he had had built with the intent of housing his third wife in, again, a forgotten mentionable. He took Charlotta back down the mountain in one of the cars used to bring the tourists from the bottom of the mountain front to The Falls because it was too rough of a terrain for drivers who were unfamiliar with navigating such roads to attempt on their own. She checked out of the room she had rented, got her clothes and permanently relocated to the mountains to be a Rastafarian mountain girl. She had lived that life for 10 years but when Franklin died, she decided that she was finally ready to go back to her real family.

In Jamaica, Charlotta had managed to find a way to live above the misery of her past and there were many quiet nights to aid her in that process. Almost every night after dinner and before Franklin would come to her for his evening rub down and a little lovemaking, Charlotta would make her way to the river's edge to sit in silence. Surrounded by the lush landscape that densely covered the jagged structure of the mountain, softening its sharpest points, and the contrasting lull of the gently moving river flowing through its middles, she'd lay in the water and allow the river to carry downstream the debris that her past had swept into her spirit.

Charlotta had a lot of time to break through the state of comfortable numbness she had slipped into the very first time her father had peeled her Barbie pajamas from her perspiring and shaking body, and she swore she'd never return to that lifeless place again. Charlotta finally realized that the family she came to call her own in that Caribbean paradise was more like the family she grew up with. But the one difference was uncanny. It was an existence that she had chosen, and that is what gave her freedom.

When she'd come home to Cincinnati, full of a peace that she'd never allow to be stolen from her again and armed with an experience developed trade that could help her to pay her bills, she was shocked to find her sisters still stuck in the listlessness of their sad reality; it was a listlessness that only marijuana, rural living, great sex with a god-built man, and total inhibition had liberated her of. She felt sorry for her sisters but freedom felt too good for her to ever retreat back inside of herself.

Floating there at that very moment made her feel a little regretful that her story was coming to its end at 55 years of age. *At least it was one hell of a story,* Charlotta thought as her invisible, ghostly vision floated down and straddled the lower, closed half of the coffin. She leaned her transparent face down into the open end, just inches from the face of the embalmed, cold outer shell she had lived in for five and half decades.

She flicked the mole on her lip and pulled at it just to see if it would come off. It looked almost plastic now. She observed her face closely, traced her full lips and slightly chubby cheeks with her fingertips and admired how flawless her skin looked, even after being frozen and stuffed. It had been a bumpy road, but she managed to stay in one piece and maintain her beauty despite the turbulent ride. All in all, she was satisfied with the way her life had turned out to be and was ready to move into her eternity without looking back or wanting any re-do's.

But just as the sun was coming up outside, awakening the last day that the world would ever glance upon her physical self again, and she would fly off into the heavens for her appointment with judgment, she took notice of how well the wig was fitting her head. She had been so distracted by memories and the get-up they had her in that it hadn't dawned on her until that very minute that her locks were far too thick and too long to fit under the contraption. She snatched the wig off so fast that some of the bobby pins that had been holding it in place went flying across the room.

She had to cover her mouth to keep from screaming, though no scream would have resounded. Her locks were gone! They had been cut down to little sprouts that almost resembled stalks of broccoli. She rubbed her fingers across the top of them and shook her head in disbelief.

Charlotta's anger went from 0 to 100 in a matter of minutes. *How could they disfigure her like this!* She yelled, again, a soundless shriek, "Those are the most simple ass women I know!" Charlotta swung her right leg over the casket and pushed her hollow, transparency to the floor. She stood there in utter amazement, staring at herself and fuming at how clueless her sisters were.

Charlotta yelled as loud as she could in her scream-less state that no one living would have heard if they had walked into the parlor of the funeral home at that very moment. "I say, fuck them all! They can't judge me ever again!"

She stifled a sob and pushed the wig back down onto the head of her corpse, briefly considering how hard her head felt and then laughed to herself as she appreciated the pun that was not intended. From the time Charlotta was three-years-old, her mother had been telling her that she didn't know how to mind.

Jorja Sweet would have said, if she had lived long enough to witness her return from Jamaica all cosmetic-less, braless, nappy headed and free that she was just being her usually hard-headed, self-absorbed self.

Charlotta could almost hear the voice of her mother telling her how stubborn she was. Standing there in her spirit state and looking at herself in her eternal stiffness, Charlotta finally gave up on trying to convince any of them to understand that all she ever wanted was to be unbound and to live outside of the walls of her prison of numbness. And once she had found her way out, she was never going back!

CHAPTER 9: ASHES TO ASHES

Merci woke up the next morning feeling more rested than she had expected. There had not been a dream the night before to interrupt her sound slumber. Merci didn't know why but she was grateful. She put on her robe and followed her nose to the kitchen where her Aunt Carmen was cooking breakfast.

"Good morning dear," Carmen spoke as the sound of Merci's footsteps entered into the room but did not turn away from the food cooking on the stove. She was turning a pan full of potatoes and onions over with one hand and with the other, pulling open the oven door to peak in on the browning biscuits that she had made from scratch.

"It smells great in here, Aunt Carmen,"

Merci eased herself into the chair closest to the stove and inhaled deeply, filling her nostrils with smells she didn't often get a whiff of in her own home. Aunt Carmen's cooking could revive an unconscious man. Merci didn't even want any coffee this morning. The aroma in the kitchen was giving her the boost she usually clung to the mug for. "But it looks like so much for only two people to eat."

"It is,' she smacked her lips and wiped her hands on the apron hanging from her hips. "I started out cooking for four people, you, me, your Aunt Camille, and Minister Bradley, but they had to cancel at the last minute. Of course, the eggs were already cracked, the dough made and the potatoes peeled." Carmen spread her arms and gestured towards the cooking food as if she were one of the Barbie-doll beauties on The Price is Right putting herself and the merchandise on display for the highest bidder.

Merci observed her aunt while Carmen went on with her rant and decided that she was a pretty woman after all, despite the weight she struggled with over the years. She was the daughter whose looks had been a perfect blend between Grey and Jorja Sweet. Who'd ever think that Grey's rough manliness and Jorja Sweet's girlie prettiness would mix so well?

Carmen was in her usually talkative mood, "Camille claims she had a rough night and needed to sleep in a little while longer. She said she'd meet us at the funeral home, never mind that I wanted her to ride with us in the family car."

Carmen's brown hair, almost the exact color of milk chocolate, swung loosely around her shoulders and outlined her face as if framed, slimming he pudgy cheeks and highlighting the softness in her lighter brown eyes. Merci thought her aunt was so much more attractive with her hair down and silently reminded herself to suggest that Carmen wear it down today.

Merci was feeling light hearted and brave, for reasons yet unfounded, but she was enjoying the place she was in this morning, and that was a far cry from where she'd been since she got here. She wasn't going to question it. She was just going to go with the wave of this mood that was shaping her morning into one she had so seldom experienced. She attempted to make Carmen feel better with a positive viewpoint.

Carmen took the bacon out of the frying pan, stirred butter into the pot of grits that sat simmering over a low fire, turned the fire out from under the potatoes and moved them to a plate lined with paper towel to soak up the excess oil, then poured the eggs right into the pan that the bacon had been cooked in, all the while talking.

"And Pastor Bradley," a softness came over Carmen's eyes and spread across her face in an all-encompassing glow as if saying the pastor's name just filled her with the Holy Ghost, "Well, Pastor is just doing his duty as the leader of his flock." Carmen was smiling brightly while she stirred the hardening eggs around in the pan.

"Sister Osbourne took ill this morning and was rushed to the emergency room. Pastor Bradley is going by the hospital to pray with her before the funeral instead of coming here to fill his belly first. Shame he couldn't make it for breakfast. A man needs nourishment before he starts a busy day."

Carmen's gaze floated to some far off place as if she

were seeing the good minister himself hovering in a bubble above her head. Merci cleared her throat and smiled a sly and knowing smile. She swore she'd heard her Aunt Carmen sigh and it tickled her to see her aunt enamored over a man.

"Earth to Aunt Carmen," she snickered and teased, "Why are you smiling so hard?"

Carmen instantly shook the dancing daydream from its bubble, "Was I smiling hard?"

She started moving the food from the counter to the table, replacing her shine with the usual compromising grin that implied she had not been rattled, moved, or affected in any way.

Merci sat watching her aunt do what she did second best to covering up the holes in her life and recalled the months she had spent there with her aunt before she left Cincinnati for college and for good. She began feeling an alien fondness in her heart for the woman who'd taken her in when Charlotta had run off.

Feeling bad for having chased her aunt's glow away and trying to recover some of the light that had faded so quickly from her aunt's expression, Merci let Carmen off the hook.

"Well, I guess it's just you and me again this morning. It's been just you and me quite a bit these last couple of days. But we've been doing all right, right?"

Carmen removed the biscuits from the oven and brushed butter across the tops of them, placed them in a basket, grabbed two plates from the cabinet and two forks from the utensil drawer, then joined Merci at the table. Carmen appeared to have detected Merci's attempt to make her feel better, and fell right into the rhythm.

"We've been doing just fine," with a smile only half recovered. Carmen grabbed the bowl of eggs and started spooning them onto her plate, then took her turn with each dish before passing them to Merci.

Silence descended on the room as they began to eat, giving Merci enough time to look ahead into the rest of her day. Again she took inventory of her emotions and delighted at the fact that she still felt unusually calm this morning, despite the task that lie ahead of delivering a eulogy for a woman she didn't really feel anything special for and that she did not know. She decided she wasn't going to think any further on the matter, deciding the words would come to her if she stopped trying so hard to find them. Instead of concentrating on matters she could not control at the moment, she decided to talk about something of less importance and more nostalgia.

"Aunt Carmen," she began, "Remember how it was before I left for college?"

Carmen glanced up at Merci, not sure where the conversation Merci was breeching would be going, especially since the only times Carmen could remember before Merci left for college were strained and stressful for her, as she found herself constantly trying to replace Charlotta. But she answered anyway.

"I remember some of those times. Why do you ask?"

"Well, that year and a half that I spent with you after Charlotta ran off to Jamaica was the most loving of times I can recall in my life." Merci smiled and reached over to pat her Aunt Carmen on the shoulder. She felt close to her aunt at that moment and hoped the gesture was enough to relay her sentiment.

Carmen was shocked and found herself at a loss for words. She really didn't comprehend how Merci could have thought those times were the most loving she had known. Sure, she had attempted to dull the heartache that Merci must have felt from the way that Charlotta had treated the child, like she didn't really like her. Sure, Carmen did her best to pick Merci up from the fall that she must have felt when Charlotta dropped the bomb on Merci about her genetic make-up on a Sunday, and then just up and left the child in the middle of the night the next Friday while Merci was out at a school function, leaving behind on her pillow a note that only said *I'm leaving and don't know when or if I'll ever be back.*

But Carmen never felt like she had ever really connected with Merci because her niece had seemed to always be so melancholy and isolated. And why shouldn't she have been quiet in her sadness? Charlotta had fed her, clothed her, and made sure she had a roof over her head, but she couldn't push beyond those basic parenting obligations to show Merci any affection, or take the time out to teach her about the changes she was experiencing in puberty. Charlotta had never shared the secrets and joys of being a woman with her one and only girl-child, the way women are supposed to share with their daughters.

In fact, Carmen couldn't remember one time when Charlotta had even hugged her baby, or held her face in admiration, or attempted to assure Merci that she was loved still and Carmen remembered this memory with a heavy heart. Merci would always say she understood that her mother needed to get away. She always sympathized with Charlotta as being as equally victimized as she had victimized Merci. Carmen's unusual silence didn't sway Merci's good mood. She continued to reminisce.

"I remember coming home from school one day feeling scattered and unsure of myself after my counselor told me that I should pursue a career like nursing, one that would guarantee a job and security to a Black woman, as opposed to trying to be a writer like I'd expressed I wanted to be. She actually had the gall to say to me that Black writers were not in demand because they simply did not have the kinds of stories that other people could relate to."

Carmen did recall that day. Merci had fallen into the foyer of her house, sobbing hysterically and flailing her arms around like a drowning swimmer, completely distraught. Being the Ms. Fix-it-All that Carmen was expected to be, she immediately sprung into "don't worry, I got this" action. She had made Merci her favorite meal that night, spaghetti and meatballs with garlic bread and salad and had decided to give Merci one of the four graduation gifts she hadn't planned to give her for another three months.

It was a placard that had a quote by Harriett Tubman engraved in gold, cursive letters: *Every great dream begins with a dreamer. Always remember, you have within you the strength, the insight, and the passion to reach for the stars, to change the world.* Merci still had the placard in her possession today. It hung on a wall in her office right in between her Bachelor's degree from The University of Maryland and her Master's Degree from NYU.

While the pasta drained and the sauce for the meatballs simmered, Carmen had called Merci into the kitchen that fateful evening so long ago, and offered her some advice. She took Merci's hands into her own before sharing her sage advice.

"In your life, there will always be people who will look at you but never see your potential, only the color of your skin. But the world moves aside to let anyone pass who knows where he or she is going. You hold on to your dream child, you can be whatever you want to be."

It had been a cliché of sorts, but it was the best Carmen could come up with, having never had any dreams of her own, or any daughters of her own to give advice to.

"You were so sweet to me, Aunt Carmen, and I never forgot the message you conveyed. It was simple, but I appreciated the time you took to make me feel better, and it turned out to be so true."

Merci was finishing her breakfast and beaming now, with the kind of smile she hadn't been able to display in years. "Did you know that I went back to the counselor the next day and told her exactly what you said to me? The look on her face was all the confirmation I needed that you were right."

Carmen was starting to be affected by Merci's sunshiny demeanor. A smile began to form across her face too and for a few minutes the air in the room was soft and palpable. Carmen inhaled the smell of the sweetness in the air and returned Merci's previous gesture with an out of place gesture of her own. She stood up and walked behind Merci, then embraced her around the shoulders in a hug that said everything that was left to be said. There was the feeling of love in her house again, and Carmen was moved to silent, yet happy tears.

Two days before, Merci would have eased out of the hold of that hug Carmen had her in, and retreated back into her safety zone where emotions were not allowed. But today, she let her aunt hold on to her and relished in the feeling of belonging that had coasted in on the current of the tangible air in the room.

****

As they pulled up to the funeral home in the family car, still basking in the elation of the morning, Merci and Carmen were holding hands. It was strange and unfamiliar, but both women had inwardly decided to go with the flow of things. And it actually felt pretty good to both of them. They damn near skipped to the front door and floated inside on the vibe.

Pastor Bradley was already there, standing at the back of the room and speaking to Ms. Carnes in hushed undertones common for the occasion. Carmen walked slightly ahead of Merci as they entered the room where the funeral would take place, but their hands were still clasped together. Pastor Elliott Bradley nodded in their direction, finished whatever he had been in the midst of saying to Ms. Carnes and walked over to them, extending his arms as he approached.

"Sister Carmen, so good to see you in such good spirits this morning. And this beautiful young sister standing next to you must be Merci."

The pastor had a deep, baritone voice that made Merci think of Barry White. She could tell that in his younger days, he had been a lady-killer. His low-cut, salt and pepper mustache accented full, brown lips and matched the salted patches that had grown in right along his hairline at his temples. His complexion, smooth and peanut butter in hue, looked as if he was a frequent patron at the spa's facial station. He smiled the most mesmerizing smile as he pulled Carmen close and rubbed her back in consolation.

Carmen finally released Merci's hand so that she could wrap both arms around the minister. She secretly fantasized about this man some nights, but always pushed the feelings away out of guilt for longing for a man of the cloth. Pulling back from his embrace, Carmen cleared her throat and tried to regain her composure while mindlessly fanning her hand towards her face to cool the rush of heat that had climbed up onto her neck. The pastor's hand resting on Carmen's shoulder almost made her tingle.

"Uh, yes," she stammered. "This is Charlotta's daughter, Merci." It was the only response that

Carmen could muster while she tried to get her run amok lust for Pastor Bradley in check.

"Sister Merci, I'm sorry for your lose. I didn't know your mother well, but if she was anything like her sister, I'm sure she was a saint," Pastor Bradley flashed his award winning smile in Carmen's direction, still holding onto Carmen's shoulders.

Carmen looked as if she'd float to the rafters of the building if he had not been holding her down. Merci eyed her aunt as she blushed. Pastor Bradley removed his hand from Carmen's shoulder and reached out to shake Merci's hand. Carmen's elation melted some as his hand slipped away and Merci inwardly laughed at the obvious affect that he was having on her aunt.

"Well, I don't know if you could call my mother a saint, but I'd venture to say that she had a good heart, even though others couldn't always see it."

The comment, obviously referring to her family, came up and out before Merci even realized she was going to say it. But not wanting to put a damper on the morning they had shared, Merci quickly recovered. "Then again, Charlotta Samuel wasn't one to brag about who she was."

"Well, God knows what lies in the hearts of those who hold their tongues." Pastor Bradley remarked with the wisdom of a seasoned minister.

"Huh, I wouldn't say Charlotta was the kind of woman to hold her tongue!" Carmen snorted a laugh as ornery as farting loudly in public and interrupted the ethereal feeling that the pastor's words were meant to impart.

Pastor Bradley, poised with a good and Godly response like any righteous minister would be, smoothly responded. "Now, Sister Carmen, if she spoke truth then you know we have to let every tongue profess." Carmen squirmed under the pastor's gentle chastising.

Merci decided that she liked him, at least in comparison to any other minister she had known in her lifetime. She wasn't big on religion, but his words were comforting to her and she received them for the earnestness with which they were given.

"Thank you for your condolences and for your words of encouragement, Pastor Bradley."

Merci shook the minister's hand one more time and left him there with her aunt so that Carmen could get back to ogling over the pastor. She made a beeline towards Ms. Carnes who was standing in the foyer and joined her in greeting the funeral attendees as they arrived. With a new sense of courage, she felt ready to get on with the matters of the day, and she now had an idea of how she was going to approach the task at hand.

By 11:30, the wake was in full swing. The funeral home was filling up with people from the church and the neighborhood coming to pay their last respects to Charlotta, a woman they had known as a child, had shunned when she was a young woman, and had seen only a few times since her return to the neighborhood ten years before.

Merci sat very still in the second row of seats and observed the faces of the funeral attendees one by one, as they walked to the front of the room and viewed the body of her mother. Some of them were unfamiliar and some were the obvious descendants of those whom she remembered before she'd left. Some of them whispered their condolences as they passed by the chair she was sitting in on their way to their own seats. Some of them lingered for a few extra seconds to share a memory they had had of Charlotta when she was a child singing in the Little Angels choir. Some of them stood at the casket and commented on how pretty Charlotta had been made up. But not one of them seemed to be in mourning. They only seemed to be there to partake in the spectacle everyone assumed was about to take place.

Merci began to fidget in her seat from the anticipation of what she was getting ready to say to address the congregation, those who had called themselves neighbors to her family but who had been less than neighborly. She couldn't believe how she had fretted over this eulogy. What had she been so afraid of? These people came to hear the truth and that's exactly what she was ready to tell them. After years of silence, she was ready to shatter the quiet wonderings that many of the people there had come to regard her family with. According to Pastor Bradley, the hearts of the quiet are still heard by God and now everyone there would hear it too. It seemed so clear to her now as she sat there returning the fake smiles spread across their faces. If they were there for drama, Merci intended to make sure that they got exactly what they had come for.

Merci heard a clock in a distant part of the funeral home strike twelve times to signal the arrival of the noon hour. She watched the people take their seats, watched Pastor Bradley take his place at the podium, watched her aunt shake a few more hands and then take the seat next to hers, and watched Ms. Carnes pass out the last few programs, usher the stragglers to their seats, then pull the doors of the room closed in preparation for the service.

One of the late arrivers happened to be her Aunt Camille. She dragged herself in looking wrinkled and disheveled, in slacks and a sports jacket like she was a double for Phillip Michael Thomas, one of the leading men from the 1980's primetime drama Miami Vice. And Merci could tell by the glossy overlay across the irises and whites of her eyes that she wasn't feeling much of anything, especially pain. Camille slumped into a seat in the same row as Merci and Carmen, but separated herself from them by a few seats. She struggled to keep her head up and it bobbed forward a couple of times from the mind altering effects of whatever pill she had taken before she was finally able to let it fall in her bosom, where it rested for what seemed like it could stay forever. Carmen just shook her head and ignored Camille as much as she could.

Merci's fidgeting had subsided and was now just the occasional shifting back and forth from one buttock to the other. The soothing tone of Pastor Bradley's voice stating the purpose of the day's gathering brought calm over Merci's anxious nerves. She allowed herself to be drawn into the tenderness of his words while he prayed and asked God to be present for the family of the deceased. His 'amen' was the last thing she focused on, instead she concentrated her attention on the face of her mother stretched out in the pearl colored casket almost directly in front of her, promising under her breath the whole time that she would give Charlotta justice today.

Merci only half listened as the choir sang an A and B selection. She heard only snatches of the obituary that Carmen read aloud while the congregation followed along, and just as the last sentence was being recited, she uncrossed her legs preparing herself to stand up, knowing that her time at the podium was coming up next. She blinked and swallowed, and then the pastor was calling her to join him at the front of the room.

Her body moved as if it were possessed, without her effort and without her control. Merci knew her legs were under her, but she couldn't really feel them on account of the tingling along her spine. She stood at the podium, at first, with her head down and in total silence. The congregation respected her moment of quiet, assuming that she was trying to find her voice in the midst of her sorrow.

But Merci's pause had more to do with dramatics. She wanted them to writhe a little longer in their hunger for something juicy. She knew that most of the people there who knew the Samuel family history were salivating in anticipation of her remarks and it mischievously excited her to know that she held their attention so intensely. She wanted the story that they would retell amongst one another for the next ten years to have its own built-in special effects so that they wouldn't have to stretch any parts into a lie. Head still bowed, Merci's voice came out of nowhere, and startled a few of the people who were inadvertently sitting on the edges of their chairs not wanting to miss one single word that came out of her mouth whenever she began to speak.

"Pastor Bradley said something to me this morning about tongues professing truths," she shifted her bowed head to her right at the man she had so quickly become so fond of and he flashed her a smile with only half of its normal brilliance.

"Well, the truth is all I know to tell today." Merci raised her head to face the crowd for the first time, and she imagined she heard a unanimous gasp rise in the room, but she knew it was most likely in her mind. With stiffening backs, some of the members in the congregation grabbed hold of the sides of their chairs as if bracing themselves against a strong wind. Merci continued.

"All eyes are on me today. Doesn't seem too different from the way it was before I moved away from here. But here I am again enduring your stares of pity and some of contempt, the prodigal child of the prodigal daughter coming home to roost. And here is Charlotta Samuel's body," she pointed directly at the casket so that every eye followed her finger to Charlotta's face, "laying in wait of its final resting place, to be finally and forever shielded from the very same eyes that could barely be taken off of her all her life and off of me right now."

The comment made the whole congregation shift their eyes back in Merci's direction and Carmen's entire body was beginning to be filled limb by limb with the kind of stress that resembled paralysis with every word that Merci spoke. She could tell by the extremely controlled way her niece was speaking that some things were about to be said that she'd find herself trying to sweep under rugs for years to come.

"I struggled for the last few days about how to address you here today. I still didn't really know verbatim what I would say, even as my body involuntarily made its way to this podium. I just knew I had to speak truth." A single tear fell from Merci's eye, but not having weight heavy enough to make it over her cheek and down her chin it sat drying in the middle of her face as if it had been tattooed there.

"Charlotta Samuel never hurt a single person, at least not on purpose. She may have been somewhat flighty, sometimes unfocused like a gypsy high on acid, she may have seemed aloof and peculiar to some of you, and surely unconventionally untraditional to most, but she was a victim. As much as some of you loathed the filth that she made real, that my growing in her belly made real for you, she was still a victim. And the moment she freed herself from the shackles of shame that bound her heart and made her spirit heavy, you all cursed her and deemed her certifiably crazy. You talked about the shame of it all, you talked about her and about me, but you never once talked *to* her, to any of us."

Merci's hands started shaking, not because she was nervous, but because an incredible energy was being unleashed in her that she had never before felt, and it had a bar-none force. It had her in its grip and she wasn't trying to break free of it.

"I believe that if any one of you, knowing what she was suffering through, had ever pulled her into your arms to hug her, bothered to love her, tell her that she was not some two-headed creature on display, that what happened to her was not her fault, nor was it normal, nor was it okay, that she would have been able to have some sense of how to love me, hell, to love herself."

She eyed the faces of each and every person hard, and delighted at the sights of their skins turning pale, and gaping mouths unable to close due to the bowl-full of shock they were being served.

"But instead you shunned her, made her feel dirty, unclean and unable to be cleansed. Instead, you cowered in your own shame, afraid to admit that somewhere along the trail of your own bloodlines the same exact thing had probably occurred. Instead, your sad ignorance stunted her emotionally and spiritually, so much so that she had to go halfway around the world to find the peace you all played "keep away from Charlotta" with." Merci's tempo and tone were slowly increasing. "She was a child, and let me just say again so you don't forget, she was a victim."

Carmen stood up suddenly, but held her place next to her chair, holding onto to the mid-rising back of the seat in front of her to steady herself from falling over. She attempted a weak effort at asserting her authority, only self-visualized and mostly unacknowledged.

"Merci, dear, this is supposed to be a eulogy, not an

attack on the good people who came here to share in your time of loss. Please don't do this," she was almost begging. And the head of every spectator snapped in her direction.

"Share? Ha! Really? Because I thought they came to witness just one more hot gossip item to add to their already fully stocked collections about the Samuel saga!"

Merci was on a roll and for all the staged melodramatics she had been trying to perform in the beginning of her soliloquy, her intent at her best Betty Davis impersonation was now forsaking her. Merci's words were showing the evidence that she was becoming un-glued. Fighting to keep her emotions under control, Merci grabbed the sides of the podium and bent her head again. She inhaled and held her breath inside for a few seconds, then exhaled very slowly.

Camille, slowly coming out of her stupor, proclaimed out of nowhere, "Let her speak."

It was all that Camille needed to say to startle the crowd and cause all heads to snap in her direction, resembling participants at a basketball game following the man with the ball up and down the court, and to send Carmen plopping back into her seat with pouted lips and steaming temples.

"Speak, Merci, speak on!" At that moment, Merci

thought that her Aunt Camille looked like she could be reenacting the scene in The Color Purple where Sophia is robustly and miraculously revived from a fifteen-year state of brokenness, stalling Carmen's ill-attempted effort at saving face. Her need to fix this particular disaster developing right before her eyes was defeated as quickly as her nerve to even try had arisen.

Camille had slowly become lucid while no one noticed, and though somewhat slurred her demand was clearly noted. Merci bore her stare into the very pupils of her aunt's glazed eyes, and without missing a beat with a blink or an inhale, she spoke more words to this woman who she'd barely spoken to in her life.

"Thank you for bothering to wake up, Aunt Camille. But your assistance is *not* needed *or* required. You hauled your raggedy, incoherent self in here today but are no less guilty than the rest of these people for wanting to be here for all the wrong reasons, so please don't try to save me now."

Camille matched Merci's stare with equivalent repugnance. "Look, you run-a-way, ill-bred hussy, I'm trying to be on your side. You don't want to start trading insults with me because you will not win. I got some hair-raising truths stored up in me too, enough to blow the entire roof off this building."

Camille sat, perched on the end of her chair looking suddenly alert and equipped for a battle by the time the last word flew from her lips. But Merci had every intention on shutting this spectacle down.

"Yes, but I don't believe I indicated to you that I needed you to be on my side. Never have been, why start now? I've been taking care of myself damn near my entire life. So quite frankly, you are irrelevant to my well-being. Now you can stay and be quiet or leave. Those are your choices. Choose now."

All eyes shifted again from Mercy to Camille, waiting to see if there would be a comeback. Camille would not be the one to disappoint. A sneering smile crept slowly onto her lips and, unsurprising to everyone there, Camille responded with amusement.

"Well all right then Merci, let me know you have some balls. Mine are bigger but I respect your ass right now. She slid back into her seat, before finishing with a bang. "Fuck you though."

Ms. Carnes, who had been standing at the back of the room, watching the fiasco take shape with absolute revulsion, started down the aisle in a mad dash that would have put Jackie Joyner to shame. Through clenched teeth and locked jaw, her words pierced the air like the venom of a deadly serpent.

"Not here, not today! You all will not destroy the reputation of this funeral home. Something told me yesterday, after overhearing the prelude to this soap opera, that you all would be trouble!"

It was odd to see this thin-framed woman, somewhat rubbery in her movements like Popeye's girlfriend, Olive Oil, otherwise prim in her demeanor marching down the aisle like a female bull on her period, headed straight for Merci, and screaming.

"If your mixed-up family wants to expose all of the sordid details of your mixed-up lives, you will be doing it on the other side of these front doors!" Every single eye looked on.

Merci raised her hand and spoke in a way that could have silenced the noisiest room, "Something must have given you all the impression that I was finished speaking."

Ms. Carnes froze in her tracks, fearing that the unstableness she heard in Merci's voice would rattle completely loose if she moved another inch.

"That's right, Ms. Carnes, back it right on up, right now! We paid for the use of your precious funeral home and we intend to be here until the very last second of our paid time ticks away! So I suggest that you march yourself right on back to where you were or the reputation of this funeral home will be the *last* thing you'll have to worry about."

Hearing Merci's threat of violence, Pastor Bradley

had finally had enough. He stood up, raised both hands over his head, signaling a silent call for order among his flock.

"I know that the congregation of Greater Good Baptist knows better than to disrespect the deceased."

There was distress overlaying the silkiness in the voice Merci had grown to love just one hour ago. "We are laying a soul to rest, not just burying a body. We cannot send her home, back to the one from which she came, with this torn and tattered baggage."

He pulled his arms back to his sides and though in an "at rest" stance, he had lost none of his authority. "Now, we have a service to continue and when I sit back in this seat, I know that's exactly what will commence."

Pastor Bradley didn't yell, he hadn't called their Christianity into question or threatened any retaliation by God if his command was ignored. He barely wrinkled the surface of his smooth skin, but every person within the sound of his voice knew that Pastor Bradley meant to be taken seriously.

Merci suddenly felt apologetic. She looked out, this time over the heads instead of at the faces of the parishioners, and directly at the cross on the back wall hanging over the doors and perfectly centered in the backdrop of Ms. Carnes' head. She was sure if she had just experienced God's presence in her spirit for the first time ever or if she just really wanted to be done with everything, but Merci's bad mood subsided. Unexpectedly calmed again and ready to re-enter this exchange with the composure she initially intended Merci cleared her throat and began speaking again in a less accusatory tone.

"I need to ask you all to forgive me for letting my anger possess me to the point of judging how you chose to protect yourselves from the earthquake brought on by my family, and the all-encompassing shadow that was cast by Grey Samuel. I want to apologize to Charlotta. Even if she was difficult to understand, I agree with the pastor that we all deserve a proper goodbye."

Merci paused to make sure that the congregation had shifted with her before continuing. "Grey Samuel, he'd be the one person I'd consider an exception to this rule. This man controlled the course of our lives…all of our lives…too long for any of us to even pinpoint the exact moment his control materialized. Today is about truth, yes, but in truth, there has to be a place for healing. Please allow me to start again."

Merci was smiling now, not yet a fully uninhibited smile, but a recognizable curl to her lips. "Today is about giving you a glimpse into the part of Charlotta you didn't know and insight about what none of us even cared to find out about."

Merci's spirit was gradually being released from its stronghold and she began a monologue so poetic in its flow, so skillful in its structure that it could have easily been considered as a work fit for any compilation of the renowned orators Merci so loved; Nikki Giovanni, James Baldwin and Toni Morrison.

"Charlotta Samuel was...*is*...more than a victim." Merci looked out over the congregation of faces, not all of whom she could put names to but that were poignantly more familiar to her than she had wished the years and distance were able to erase. Not mere or distant enough for Merci, she again pushed their faces out of her focus and delivered the rest of the eulogy she had begun, but this time absent of the warring tone it had held before.

"You, whom Charlotta Samuel knew all her life; who knew her, who knew her mother Jorja Sweet before her, who knew our family and our circumstance. You knew us in our imagined and ill-fated glory, and had ring side seats for our fall from grace."

Merci swallowed hard to clear her throat, then continued, "What can I say that you don't already know, already think you know, or haven't already talked into knowing?"

Merci didn't know word for word what was coming next but continued anyway. "So again, here we are…me trying to figure out how to say what we all need to hear to bring clarity and closure to the life that has ended, you waiting to hear how it's going to be done. Allow me to tell you who she was, who she is, and always will be."

In its fully manifested form now, Merci's smile impelled her face to glow and that calm she had awaken to this morning had been mercifully handed back to her from a place she acknowledged as luck, but what a more spiritual woman might have interpreted as God's grace.

The poetry continued, "Charlotta Samuel, a woman who learned to love her unique attributes and live her life with no excuses and no regrets. From compromising through internalizing, and finally to self-realizing, she understood the perfection of being imperfect. We could have all benefited if we had taken the time to stand back, watch and learn from her. She, like the hardened, weather dried parts of the mountain she lived on in Jamaica, did not whine because somewhere, at that very moment that she was standing on the rugged landscape of that mountain, someone else was in the meadows of that same mountain enjoying downpours of showers that made the flowers bloom, and made the trees lush and green."

"Charlotta did not complain about the jagged edges in her life, maybe that's why *we* never bothered to ask her how she had been affected." Merci pointed her finger back and forth between her torso and then in the direction of the now entranced congregation, each and every body being swooned by Merci's eloquent ascent into this melodic composition, seemingly being spoken like the revelation of the Ten Commandments to Moses inspiring him to inscribe even as the voice of God revealed them.

"No, she did not complain about her cracked and worn parts. She discovered how to reinvent herself, look people directly in the soul and tell them in a minute that they could kiss her sun beaten behind because she was beautiful still and they could accept what she was offering or keep it moving."

Camille signified, "Uhm, hmm, just keep it moving," this time in a low, vibrating timbre that leant itself to the elevation of the poetic embrace everyone had been taken up in, instead of taking away like her previous mischief had.

"Charlotta Samuel, sometimes affected us like a long-winded epic poem, taking us on roller coasters of emotion driven by the what is, not the what ifs in life. She had a radiant, and to some, an irresistible smile that could make us aware of the best in us and eyes that could penetrate the core of the worst in us. With Charlotta Samuel, there was nothing between the lines. She lived her life by the words our hearts were afraid to speak aloud. Who we saw, or didn't see for whatever reason, was who she was 100% of the time. Now free from her earthly shell, she is a wordless poem sharing with us her resilient spirit, reminding us that we will always be changed, but we can never be reduced. And finally no longer needing to tell or be told, she will open up her silent wings and soar to her paradise."

Merci was nearing the end of her address, and believing that she had done her duty, felt a spinning in her head that bordered on ecstasy. She noticed a few people in the congregation had been moved to tears, and she knew that what she had said was well with Charlotta's soul.

"Charlotta Samuel was also granted the blessing of peace despite having been predisposed to disorder and confusion. We should all hope to someday know her peace."

Walking away with not another audible exhale coming through the overhead speakers of the room Merci took her seat in between her aunts and did not look to either of her sides. She simply motioned with a nod of her head to Pastor Bradley, letting him know that he could reclaim the attention of the audience and get on with his sermon.

Soon after, the service was ending. The pallbearers loaded Charlotta's casket into the hearse and the congregation began pouring out of the funeral home and piling into their cars, awaiting the final preparation of sticking flags onto the hoods of each car that would be in the procession to the gravesite.

Ms. Carnes was wiping her brow with the handkerchief she had squeezed in her palm the whole time, thankful that her funeral home was still standing and distributing her business card as the people passed her on their way out.

As the crowd thinned, Carmen was finally able to peel her butt from her chair. She staggered out the funeral home and to the family car looking like she had gotten into Camille's stash of "Hollywood" drugs and feeling weary from all the emotional surprises of the service.

Camille, however, had a bit of a skip in her walk that resembled more of a stride now as opposed to the sluggish slide she had come into Jordan and Jordan with. Carmen, now sulking and shaken, and Camille now buzzing with the kind of instinctive reaction we all get when things are going our way, seemed to have traded personalities like they were Dr. Jekyll and Mr. Hyde.

And Merci was feeling good and flying as high as her mother's ghost, which had floated in during the commotion and hovered in the rafters of the roof, just in time to witness with her own transparent eyes, her daughter take one step closer to her own sense of peace and sanity. It was the one thing that Charlotta had always wanted for Merci, even when she didn't know how to give it to her.

At the burial site, Merci walked right up to the pearly casket, kissed the cold cheek of her mother's spiritually hollowed, cotton stuffed frame, and began to slowly pull the hood of the casket down. A small and single tear formed at the corner of Merci's eye at the thought of seeing her mother's face for the very last time before she was lowered into the ground. But then, she thought she saw her mother's dead face smile, and with less than a corner of her cheek still in view before the casket's open door was permanently sealed, Merci smiled back at her.

This story is continued in:

Reaching the Edge of Merci: The Reckoning

Be sure to Check out other titles from B Cyde Books

Authoress Dawn Crooks

Check out more titles from B Cyde Books

**All B Cyde Books titles are available on
Amazon & Kindle**

www.ingramcontent.com/pod-product-compliance
Lightning Source LLC
Chambersburg PA
CBHW060407180626
46817CB00007B/2538